More by the Author

Horror

Dissonance Junction

From the Shadows

The Dark Collective

Granny Bael

Anthologies

Unnerving: Volumes 1—3

The Mighty Pen

Tales of the Slug

DISSONANCE JUNCTION

a year of stories

LAUREN PATZER

BLUE FORGE PRESS
Port Orchard, Washington

Dissonance Junction: A Year of Stories
Copyright © 2019, 2022
by Lauren Patzer

First eBook Edition March 2021
First Print Edition March 2021
Second Print Edition June 2022

Cover design by Brianne DiMarco
Interior design by Brianne DiMarco

ISBN 978-1-59092-870-7

For information about film, reprint or other subsidiary rights, contact: blueforgegroup@gmail.com

Blue Forge Press is the print division of the volunteer-run, federal 501(c)3 nonprofit company, Blue Legacy, founded in 1989 and dedicated to bringing light to the shadows and voice to the silence. We strive to empower storytellers across all walks of life with our four divisions: Blue Forge Press, Blue Forge Films, Blue Forge Gaming, and Blue Forge Records. Find out more at www.MyBlueLegacy.org

Blue Forge Press
7419 Ebbert Drive Southeast
Port Orchard, Washington 98367
blueforgepress@gmail.com
360-550-2071 ph.txt

To my fellow writers out there, keep at
it and don't give up hope.

There's an audience out there
for your story.

Keep perfecting your craft
and someday you will find them.

TABLE OF CONTENTS

DISSONANCE JUNCTION

a year of stories

LAUREN PATZER

 FATHERHOOD

I looked into the dark night sky, slightly emboldened that we could see the stars again after so many years. It was strange to me how a constant overcast sky could affect your mood. Behind me, Anna worked with the rags we'd scavenged, taking care of her new development—menstruation.

I'm torn between relief that she's grown up, survived in this hellscape and appears healthy and normal. The past fifteen years had been a learning experience I never thought I'd live through. I looked out from the hilltop we retreated to, watching for any signs of trackers, the humans who'd risen to the top of the wild packs due to their sense of smell, hearing or eyesight. If they found us, I'd be the next meal while Anna would become a breeder. Not that she would escape that fate anyway, but I could do my damnest to make sure it didn't happen in a tracker pack.

"I think that's it," Anna whispered, coming up behind me quietly. I honestly didn't hear her. Whether that's a testament to her stealth skills or my wandering thoughts, I didn't know. I'd like to think

I taught her well enough to sneak up or away from anything this new, desiccated world could throw at her.

I took a whiff of the air and nodded my head.

"It's barely noticeable now," I said as I turned my eyes to the north. "We need to keep moving."

"We're not making camp here?" Anna asked. There was a hint of worry in her voice. I shook my head.

"That last tracker pack was only half a day behind us," I said. "It's best we not take any chances and keep moving. We can move faster and they can't move at night as easily with a large group."

"But our chance of injury," Anna began.

"I know, but especially now, we can't risk any encounters with trackers. It will end badly for both of us."

Anna nodded and we made our way north, using the stars as our guide. After a few hours, we happened upon a complex of caves in a cliff face and I selected the one with the best chance of escape and least chance of ambush. I explained my reasoning to Anna; this passing of knowledge could be what allows her to survive where billions had perished before her.

As we settled down in the cave, she snuggled up next to me and I rested my head against the cave wall. My mind wandered back to when I first found her, sitting in the back of an SUV amidst the ruins of Vegas. How she survived with what I assumed were her dead parents in the front of the vehicle for a week after the disaster, I didn't know. She was a hardier breed than most, I supposed. My first instinct was to run. I knew there would be scavengers, wild people for whom all hope was lost and desperation the only emotion they knew. They'd come, perhaps they'd save her and take her in, but just as likely she'd meet a savage end. One look into her blue eyes and I knew I couldn't leave her there to die.

It took some wrangling with ropes and defunct power lines to create a rickety rope bridge across the chasm that had been created a week earlier when the earth's crust had been torn asunder. I worried she would cry out and fuss, drawing unwelcome eyes to our situation, but she remained silent, watching me work my way to her. That patience and ability to keep quiet contributed to our survival all these years.

I fell into a fitful sleep until shortly before dawn when rodent activity alerted me to the ending night. Anna was already awake and had caught two wood rats. I heard the fire crackling from deep inside the cave, but didn't smell anything or see smoke. My lessons on how to stay hidden were well absorbed by my young protégé.

I moved deeper into the cave and found a larger cavern that could capture and hold the smoke, at least until it could filter out through the fissures in the granite and limestone above our heads. Anna was on the far side of the cavern, deeper into the cliffside. I noticed she used some of the herbs and plants we gathered along our travels. The thin metal pot we scavenged years ago still functioned well for most of our cooking and water sterilization needs. I noticed the rats had been skinned and dangled over the fire at just the right distance, impaled on thick wooden sticks. All of this reminded me in a flash that, if I were to succumb to some illness or mishap with wild life or the even worse and more ruthless human adversary, Anna would survive if she could escape.

We ate in silence. Anna read from one of the many books we scavenged from a school years ago. It was simple and elementary, but I'm relieved to see she enjoyed consuming the written word. I can only hope she'd taken in enough with my impromptu instruction to someday produce content or at least pass on the skills to her offspring.

"What are these?" Anna handed me the kindergarten book we found just weeks ago. It was the first time she'd opened it. I looked at the flying machine and understood why she didn't recognize it. She'd never seen one flying through the air unless she'd possibly noticed one before the cataclysm. Even then, she probably wouldn't remember them.

"Airplane," I said.

"I know how to read the word airplane, but I don't understand what the object is," Anna said. She chewed thoughtfully on a bit of wood rat meat seasoned with dandelions and chicory. "What does it do?"

"They flew through the air, transporting people long distances," I said. She didn't look convinced.

"Like magic? I thought you said there was no such thing as magic." Anna drank some dandelion tea and looked at me expectantly.

"It was a machine that used scientific principles like lift, air flow, wing design and jet propulsion to rise into the air." I shrugged my shoulders. "I don't have a scientific background, so I can't explain exactly how that worked. It was like the cars except it traveled through the air."

"The cars." Anna raised her eyebrows. "They still sound like magic to me."

"I know," I said. I looked at the fire and realized it may make the lesson a little easier to understand. "You know how there is something rising from the water when you make it hot?"

"Steed?" Anna said and frowned.

"Close, it's steam." I pointed at the pot of tea she had made. "That steam rises. Some people know how to harness that action, capture that energy and use it to run an engine or mechanism."

"Why?" Anna asked. She was intent on my every word, so hungry for knowledge I could barely provide to her.

"It's a tool for accomplishing something with better efficiency than can be accomplished with one person's or even many people's power and energy."

Anna nodded her head.

"Like the bow and arrow is more efficient for hunting and the snare is more effective at catching small game than running around trying to smash them with a rock." She looked at me and smiled.

"Well," I said. "I didn't expect you'd remember that particular hunting lesson word for word."

"I went hungry that night and that's a great memory maker," she said.

"We went hungry and it's a great way to remember," I corrected. "OK, so we may find someone where we're going that has tools running on steam or something else. It's good you're aware of what machines are."

"Where are we going?" Anna said as she began to pack up our foodstuff and cooking utensils.

"You remember the old man we came upon last winter?"

"He died," Anna said. There was no emotional component to the statement, but it still jarred me. My old sensibilities still grieved for the loss of human life, even more so given the devastation that appeared to happen to the human race. It seemed like every loss of life now was another nail in the coffin for humanity.

"He did, but before he died, he mentioned a friend of mine. At least, I'm hoping it's my friend and not someone else. Daniel Casson. You remember?"

Anna nodded and stood up. She finished packing.

"Time to check for safety," she said. I nodded. We ended the conversation and we both crept to the front of the cave and looked out. I saw a thin column of smoke rising far in the distance. I waited for Anna's assessment.

"Nothing close," she whispered. She nodded in the direction

of the smoke. "The tracker camp is behind us and a bit off to the right."

"Which means?" I asked.

"They've likely lost our trail," Anna said. "We should continue to head away from their camp and put more distance between us to ensure we don't run into them."

"Perfect," I said. Anna smiled at me for the compliment of her abilities. I saw at that moment that she had indeed grown up before my eyes into an attractive woman. My heart swelled a little and then darkened. If we met strangers in the wild, her maturity was a liability to her and to me as well. She wasn't just another mouth to feed as she had been before. Now she was an asset as well as an object of desire for breeding and other things.

"Best we get moving as quickly as possible," I said. Anna and I both crawled carefully from the mouth of the cave, still watching the surrounding landscape for any signs of movement. There were none and we completed our exit and descended back into the high brush surrounding the rise.

Travel over land was as fast as we could possibly make it. Our northward trek didn't seem to concern my companion as much as it did me. She'd never seen summer on the plains. It was still spring, so the heat wouldn't be sweltering yet. As we walked I thought about the wisdom of my musings and realized I was projecting pre-cataclysm memories on the environment. In truth, I didn't know what the northern climes would bring in terms of weather anymore.

We passed by what I remembered as Yellowstone. For two weeks, a collection of charred daggers pushed up through the earth into the sky. The disappearance of cloud cover might regenerate the barren landscape, but I wasn't hopeful. Most vegetation higher than three feet barely clung to life through the last fifteen years. A suddenly rejuvenated forest would take decades but might never happen in this area. I didn't think I'd see a lush forest again, at least not in my lifetime.

Halfway through the wilderness, we came upon the tell tale signs of an old road. I stopped and pulled out an ages old map. Unfolding it carefully, I did some triangulation with the forest and the road. I figured it was state route 20. The old man said Daniel was somewhere south of what used to be Billings. I did my best estimation and changed our trajectory. I showed Anna what I'd done even though the landmarks of old would be lost on her. Maybe someday she'd teach the next generation how to make maps.

As the weeks of travel dragged on, Anna got a better handle on handling her monthly visitor. We approached a large rock outcropping that somewhat resembled a mountain that had broken through the earth's crust. I recognized the two-story high walls built from gravel surrounding and blocking off most of the path to the mountain, just like the old man described it. This would lead into a labyrinth of sorts—a defensive configuration meant to slow down attackers and put them at the mercy of defenders. I wondered how Daniel had managed it; it was an enormous amount of earth to move without the benefit of bulldozers and dump trucks.

"Keep your weapons stowed," I reminded Anna. "We wouldn't survive an attack even if we had them out."

"Don't provoke them," Anna said, nodding.

We walked to the edge of the first wall. I heard sounds above us, but the echoing confused my senses and I was never sure where our observers were exactly, which was just the way they wanted it. As we moved into the interior, we had to pass through gaps barely large enough for a single person, again defensive design meant to slow down anyone entering the labyrinth. All the while, the sounds of moving rocks above us meant our progress was being monitored closely.

When we finally emerged from the six interlocked walls of rock that made up the labyrinth, we came to an array of construction machines. After so many years, they no longer had usable tires and rested on tire debris mashed under the rims. Looking at the array of machinery, I understood how they moved so much earth and rock to make the walls behind us. Arrayed in a semi-circle around the exit from the labyrinth, I could also tell this was yet another defensive position for Dennis' home base. Depending on the number of people he had inside, I could see the defensive corridor he'd setup could repel an incredibly large number of invaders. I don't think I'd seen a tracker pack large enough to make it past the labyrinth much less this next line of defense. I hadn't seen any weapons yet, but even the heavy rocks thrown down from above would damage or kill most would be invaders. Perhaps this last line was where the projectile weapons would come into play or some other weapon I hadn't considered yet.

High above our heads, in the cab of a large earth mover I'd only seen in mining quarries before, sat a man with long dark hair observing us. He waved.

"Hank?" the man shouted down to us.

"Howard Ferber, but my friends called me Hank years ago," I replied.

"Friends?!" the man said as he laughed, "I don't recall you having any of those!"

"Dennis, I presume," I replied.

"Probably," the man responded, not moving from his perch. As I watched him, I noticed several heads appearing between the crevices of the machinery in front of us, wielding what looked like bows and arrows. "You'll have to forgive my caution. We don't get many visitors that don't wish us harm or want to take what we've built here."

"Understood. I come wishing only peace." I bowed. "And perhaps a bit of Jamaican jerky?"

The man nodded. "That's something Hank would say, but also something that could be tortured out of him." He stepped out of the cab onto the surrounding decking. I noticed the age lines now and the graying hair. He was in his forties like me. "What was the first course we took together at Antioch?"

"English Lit, but it wasn't at Antioch, it was at Villanova. Third class of the day."

"Correct. And the teacher's assistant's name?"

"Frederica. Her sister wound up being your wife."

Daniel began to climb down the steps of the mammoth vehicle.

"She was indeed."

"I'm sorry," I said.

"It was another time, another place," Daniel said as he hit the ground. "Another world, really."

Daniel walked up to me. Involuntarily, I stepped back with a barely perceptible flinch. He didn't seem to notice and just engulfed me in a hug. I awkwardly hugged him back. I'd more expected him to deck me at the least after all these years. Daniel stepped back and held me by my shoulders.

"You look like hell," Daniel said. "Come on in—we've got a spring. A cool drink will do you good."

He turned and shouted "Guardia!" Four kids moved from their perches on the equipment and ran to ramps along the sides of the immense cavern that took them up to the tops of the rock barrier walls behind us. Daniel walked forward. Anna looked at me and I nodded. I followed Daniel as another five people, three of them adults, ran ahead and into the opening in the wall that led to the interior of the immense complex.

As we passed the orange and red walls, the interior revealed itself to be more of a dark brown color. The walls appeared smooth as if polished by water, but there was none present. Daniel gestured overhead. "The remains of an aquifer the earth belched up during the event," he said.

"It's cooler than outside," I noted. Anna looked in wonder at the walls. This was completely alien to her. "An aquifer was an underground reservoir of fresh water."

"Oh," she said and continued to glance around. "Where did the water go?"

"Some of it," Daniel answered, "is still here. But the greater majority of it burned away up into the atmosphere. The rains have picked up though, so it will be coming back, but clearly it will never fill this space again as its above ground now."

We entered some winding paths in the cavern walls and came to a room where water bubbled from a hole in the wall down along a trench and into another hole where it splashed somewhere below into a larger pool of water. Daniel grabbed a cup from next to the hole and filled it up with water. The cup looked like it had been carved from stone. He handed it to me and I drank readily, closing my eyes and savoring the cleanest water that had passed my lips in over a decade. As I was gorging myself, Daniel filled another cup and handed it to Anna. She looked at me briefly and then followed suit, drinking in the precious fluid.

"So, what brings you to our humble abode?" Daniel asked. He took our cups and refilled them, handing them back to us as we drank our fill again.

"An old man let me know about this place," I said. Daniel looked down.

"Albert Foster, the only person who left us for different pastures," Daniel said. "He's dead then?"

"Yes," I said. "But how did you know?"

"It's the only way he'd let slip his knowledge of this place."

"Oh, I didn't kill him," I said quickly. Daniel laughed.

"No, he would've directed you somewhere entirely different if you'd tortured him. I suspect you saved him from some calamity, but his injuries were too severe to recover."

"Tracker pack," I said. "I flew into a rage when I saw them torturing him. Killed a few and the rest ran off. I guess I lost control that day."

Daniel nodded and then turned to Anna.

"And what's your story, miss?"

Anna looked at me and I nodded.

"My name's Anna. I travel with Howard," she said. She looked back at me and shrugged. I chuckled.

"I saved Anna when she was quite young, after the cataclysm," I said.

"Cataclysm?" Daniel raised his eyebrows. "That's a catchy term for it."

"I pulled her out of a wrecked SUV in what was left of Vegas," I said. Daniel motioned to some rock outcroppings that were the right height for sitting or even laying on. He sat and we followed his example. "Do you know what happened? I never found out."

"The reports I heard were only a few hours old before everything went to hell," Daniel said. "Drilling for oil, gas, whatever else they could find beneath the earth's crust. I guess there was some kind of offshore drilling race to claim the most of the new oil fields they'd discovered. The ocean started boiling around one of the oil rigs and then several of them. Some of the countries were using explosives and it escalated to cracking the crust just right to release a volume of magma the likes of which probably hasn't been seen since the time before the dinosaurs."

"Did they try to fix it?" I asked.

"Once that genie had been let out of the bottle, well…" Daniel shrugged. "I tried the math once and figured a quarter to a third of the Pacific ocean probably boiled away into the atmosphere. With the weight of the ocean's diminished on the floor of the ocean, that lead to the big eruption or cracking of the crust or whatever it was. Maybe four hours passed from the first signs to all hell breaking loose. I had a refuge, you know. Designed it for just this occasion."

"I remember," I said. "Didn't you call it Hell Hole?"

"Right," Daniel sighed. "I just thought I'd be using it for a political nightmare. I didn't realize the earth would fight back so hard. I survived, but just barely. Hell Hole is no more, but it served it's temporary function of keeping me alive. I emerged, surveyed what there was left of the landscape and the resources and managed to devise our little getaway here. 40 people live here now. 25 originally and as time, illness, additions and subtractions affected us, we grew to 40."

"That's less than most tracker packs," I said.

"We haven't been adding women fast enough to keep up with the attrition," Daniel said.

"I thought that might be the case," I said. "It's one of the reasons we came."

Daniel looked at Anna and then back to me. "Does she know that?" Daniel asked.

"Some, not all," I said. "It's a little complicated."

Daniel nodded.

"I'll be a breeder?" Anna asked. "That's what you're talking about, isn't it?"

"Yes, but Daniel and I aren't sure you have all the details you need to know about it. It can be a bit of a shock."

"You didn't want me to be a breeder with the tracker packs,"

Anna said. "Is being a breeder bad?"

"Uh..." I scratched my head.

"If I may," Daniel said. "All the young women learn what it means to be a breeder in consultation with Rebecca."

I breathed a sigh of relief. Being a father figure was hard enough. Explaining propagation of the human race? That was well beyond me. "If that's all right with Anna, I don't have any objections," I said.

"Okay," Anna said. "If Howard comes with me."

I nodded. "I had a feeling that would be the case."

Daniel led us through a labyrinth of tunnels until we came to a medium sized cavern. Rebecca was an older woman, in her 50s. She turned to watch us as we entered. Another young woman moved about in the cavern behind her. I noted she was with child.

"Rebecca," Daniel shouted out. "Come meet my old friend Hank and his companion Anna." Rebecca came toward us. Daniel turned back to us and smiled. "Rebecca is what we would call a midwife in the old days. She's also our primary medical expert."

Rebecca reached her hand out to shake and I reciprocated. Anna watched us both curiously. I thought I might have seen a momentary flash of jealousy cross her face. It was then that I realized we hadn't spoken with other people often, perhaps a handful of times, in all these years. All of Anna's social interaction had been primarily with me and I hadn't made much of an effort to teach her manners; most of the time, I just advised her to remain silent. But her face betrayed her thoughts.

"Welcome, Hank and Anna. It is nice to meet you both," Rebecca reached out to shake Anna's hand and Anna looked at me, waiting for a nod before she complied. "How long have you been travelling?"

"Fifteen years," I replied.

"I see," Rebecca said and looked at Anna. "How old are you, my dear?"

Anna looked at me again for permission to speak.

"Anna, you can speak freely with these people. They are friends and this will be your new home," I said. Anna's eyes didn't leave mine.

"I may be eighteen years old, maybe less, maybe more. You didn't say our new home." Anna didn't even look at Rebecca. I sighed.

"I may not be staying long," I said.

"You're welcome to stay as long as you like," Daniel said.

"Crowds," I said. "They're still a thing."

"Some things don't change," Daniel replied. He moved behind Rebecca and took a seat on a large rock. "Anna, your companion, Hank here, has had a history of being a loner. I was quite surprised to see him travelling with anyone else."

"You've always been with me," Anna said. "What did I do wrong?"

"Nothing, Anna," I said. "Now that you're a woman, it's not safe to travel with me anymore. It will be much safer for you here."

"I wish we'd never come here," Anna said. She turned to Rebecca. "Can you teach me how to not be a woman?"

Rebecca looked at me. "I'm afraid that's not how it works, Anna," Rebecca said as she returned her attention to Anna. "Time marches on, we grow older, our bodies mature and things change. Come meet Tanya." Rebecca held out her hand. Anna took it without looking at me. They walked over to the pregnant young woman and chatted with her for a while.

"You could stay," Daniel said. "Fifteen years travelling with another person is amazing. I never thought I'd see you share your life with anyone."

"I didn't feel like I had a choice," I said.

"Perhaps it's better if you don't have a choice then," Daniel chuckled. "You care for her, otherwise you would've left her to the tracker packs. You cared for someone, Hank. That's huge."

"I've been trying to find a way to let her loose the entire time, Daniel," I said. "I haven't changed except to save her life."

"That's better than you did twenty years ago," Daniel said. I didn't say anything, but I knew he was right at least in that sense. Twenty years ago, I would've left Anna to die in that car just as I'd left Frederica.

Later that night, as I lay looking at the stars through a hole in the rocks, Anna came and lay with me. A week later, I left the complex, never to see them again. I know she watched me as I entered the interleaving walls of rock, but I never looked back.

HOUSE GUEST

lyssa watched the snow fall outside. The wind whipped the flakes into a frenzy. She smiled and sighed. The new house finally felt comfortable after a few weeks of adapting to the larger floor plan, the new neighborhood and Mary's new school. Alyssa's husband, John, entered the kitchen. He frowned at something on the other side of the dining room table.

"What is it?" Alyssa asked.

"Uh," John started. He pointed at the floor. "Did Mary hurt herself?"

Alarmed, Alyssa rushed over to see what he was talking about. One of the small juice glasses that had been on the table for breakfast was on the floor, shattered. The red tinged edges of the shards of glass matched the spattered drops on the floor near the glass. A red, opaque liquid reflected brightly in the early morning sunlight.

Alyssa knelt near the glass and shook her head. "I didn't hear anything," she said. "Maybe when I let the dog out, he knocked it off the table."

"Mary, can you come here please?" John called out. In a few

seconds, the sound of footsteps on the stairs announced the approaching daughter. Her brunette curls framed a cute face as the nine-year old entered the kitchen. John pointed at the glass.

"Did you do that?" John asked.

"No." Mary frowned. "Is Max okay?"

John looked back over at the glass and noticed the drops of blood, but no paw prints.

"Max is fine," John said.

Alyssa knelt down and took Mary's hands in her own, looking for cuts. She examined her clothes for any signs of blood, but there were none.

"John," Alyssa said. "There's no blood."

As John looked down at Mary's hands, the sound of shattering glass erupted behind them and they all jumped. Another glass had been pushed from the table and there was a small puddle of blood beneath this one. Max started barking through the back door.

"What the hell?" John said. A sudden knock at the front door caused them all to jump again.

John took Mary by the hand and they walked to the front door. As they opened the door, another crash from the kitchen table made them all jump. John looked at Alyssa standing in the entry to the dining room. She turned to look at them and she was pale as the snow outside.

"There's blood dripping down the walls," Alyssa said.

"Oh, sounds like Arthur is active again," announced an old man's voice from the front doorway. They all looked to see a short, elderly gentleman dressed in slacks, white shirt, red bow tie and a tweed jacket standing there glancing in Alyssa's direction.

"And you are?" John asked.

"Alan Turtledove, your next door neighbor. Just came by to say hi and find out if your poltergeist had become active yet. I see that it has.”

Alyssa approached the door and smiled.

“Won’t you come in, Mr. Turtledove? We can sit down in the living room. I’m afraid the dining room is a bit of a mess at the moment,” Alyssa’s voice trailed off as she glanced at the area where all the broken glass and blood seemed to be accumulating.

“Don’t mind if I do,” Alan said and walked by the distracted family. He moved confidently into the living room and sat down on the far end of the couch.

John looked down at Mary; he was still holding her hand. He let go and smiled. “Go back upstairs and play,” he said and then walked into the living room where Alan nodded at him. Alyssa walked in slowly, paying more attention to the dining room than the living room.

John sat down in the dark brown leather recliner. Alyssa sat on the other end of the couch. She had the manner of one watching a super slow tennis match, glancing at Alan and then back at the dining room and back again every few seconds.

“Did you say the poltergeist was named Arthur?” John asked.

“Well,” Alan said. “That was what the previous family called him. I don’t really know if that’s his or her name, but I don’t have another to call it, so Arthur seems reasonable.”

“Reasonable... sure...” Alyssa said.

“Why is there so much blood?” John asked.

“Funny you should ask, John,” Alan said.

“I didn’t tell you my name,” John replied.

“Didn’t you?” Alan asked and then continued. “The poltergeist manifests the major sin or activity of a family member, or so it’s been described to me anyway. Are either of you a phlebotomist by chance?”

“No,” Alyssa said. “I work with animals mostly.”

"Well, I'm a medical device salesman, so maybe that's where it's getting its ideas from," John chuckled. "Too bad I'm not a banker!"

Alan nodded and smiled. "The last occupants of the home were a military family and the mother served continuous tours in Iraq and Afghanistan. When they'd come home, they'd find piles of sand all over the house."

"Well, that doesn't seem so bad," Alyssa said.

"Debatable," Alan replied. "They always had portions of human bodies sticking out of them."

"Oh my," Alyssa said.

"They figured this out the first time when they vacuumed up the first pile of sand and a disembodied finger jammed the vacuum."

"If there were dead body parts, surely they contacted the police," John said.

"Right you are," Alan said. "The first couple of times anyway."

"What happened?" Alyssa was paying full attention to Alan now.

"Every time they'd clean up the sand, it would mysteriously disappear from the vacuum cleaner bag. Same thing with the body parts; no matter where they put them or even left them where they lay, as soon as the police arrived, they'd disappear," Alan said. He leaned back in the couch. "This is probably the most comfortable couch I've ever sat in."

"So," John said as he sat forward in the chair. "Did the poltergeist stop?"

"Oh sure, after a couple of years," Alan said. "When they arrested the mother for her involvement in a body parts black market ring."

"What?" Alyssa said, her eyes wide.

"She was shipping bodies back on ice from the different

countries she was stationed in," Alan said. "So you both travel for your jobs? Very convenient."

"How do you know that?" Alyssa asked this time. Her tone changed in an instant to dark and demanding.

"Alright, Mister Turtledove, I think we've played enough parlor games for one day," John said, standing up. "I'll see you to the door."

Alan raised his eyebrows and smiled.

"Of course, if you have any questions, I live right next door," Alan pointed south and stood up. He shuffled to the front door as John and Alyssa glanced at one another, concern on their faces.

"Perhaps we'll see you tomorrow," Alyssa said. She had joined John a few steps behind Alan.

Alan stepped out the door, stopped and turned around. "Oh, you'll have so much more to worry about before tomorrow comes," Alan said. He turned away from them and walked through the snow toward what they assumed was his house. Alyssa glanced down and grabbed John's arm.

"Look!" she said and pointed at the snow. The snow surface was pristine where Alan had walked leaving not a single footprint. As they looked down and then back up, their strange visitor had disappeared from sight.

"Parlor tricks," John murmured. He walked back into the house. He stopped in the door frame, looked back at Alyssa and smiled. "I work with animals? Nice."

Alyssa looked down and frowned. "I thought it was more clever than medical device salesman." Alyssa looked up and examined the surrounding neighborhood. After a few moments, she turned and followed John into the house.

John was in the kitchen, looking in the corners of the ceilings in the dining room. Alyssa walked in and shook her head.

"You think I didn't check before we purchased the house?" Alyssa chided.

John walked out in the living room, still looking up.

"It's amazing what they can do with technology nowadays," John replied. He looked down at his watch and touched the screen a few times. The display changed to reflect different measurements. "If it's a psychedelic, it's not registering in the bloodstream."

Alyssa passed John and let the dog in. She pointed at the place Alan had been seated. The dog went over to the sofa, sniffed it a few times, put his tail between his legs and went directly to his dog bed by the back door. Alyssa and John blinked for a few moments and then looked at each other.

"What the hell does that mean?" John asked.

"Can I have some juice?" Mary said from behind them, causing them both to jump slightly. Alyssa rushed over to her.

"Of course, sweetie," Alyssa said and walked into the kitchen with Mary. John kneeled down next to Max and patted him on the head. Max continued to whimper. John snapped his fingers and pointed at the couch. Max put his head down and refused to move. John looked over at the place where Alan sat earlier and frowned.

He grabbed his coat and walked out the door. He stomped through the snow, which gave way beneath his feet leaving a clear trail behind him as he journeyed to the neighbor's house. He stepped up on the porch as the daylight began to fade and knocked on the door. After a few moments, a young woman came to the door.

"Yes?" she asked as she smoothed her apron. John noted a bit of flour on her cheek and dusting her clothes.

"Hi, I'm your new neighbor," John said and pointed back toward his house. "I had a chat with Alan earlier and was wondering if I could speak with him again."

"Uh…" The woman frowned. "It's just me and my husband

Randall here."

"Is Randall an older man with white hair?"

"No," she said, laughing. "He's three years older than me, but his hair is even darker than mine." She pointed at her brunette locks.

"Do you have a houseguest named Alan?"

"No." She looked back into the house and then turned again toward John. "The man who owned this house before us was named Alan. I think his last name was Turner something."

"Turtledove?" John asked.

"Yes," she replied, brightening. "That's it."

"Would you have contact information for Mister Turtledove?"

"Oh." The woman looked down. "I'm afraid we got the house at an estate auction. Mr. Turtledove passed away last year."

John whipped out his cell phone and performed a few quick searches on the internet, finding an obituary for Alan Turtledove. The picture matched their visitor from just a few minutes ago.

John smiled at the woman. "I'm sorry for the intrusion. Thank you for your time." He nodded his head and turned around, walking on the shoveled path to the sidewalk. He glanced at the snow he'd walked on earlier and saw just his footsteps. He walked around the block, looking for unusual vehicles or random pedestrians that shouldn't be there or anything else out of the ordinary. It was depressingly normal. He returned to his house and walked in the front door.

"Alyssa?" John called out.

"Mommy's up here," Mary replied. John walked up the stairs, smiling at Mary who waited at the top of the staircase. When he got eye to eye with Mary, the knife in her hand glided through the air so quickly, he didn't even see it before it sunk into his jugular. He was so shocked that he staggered backward and fell down the stairs. His neck broke and the life was snuffed from him before he could bleed to death.

Mary sat down on the top stair and looked down at the man she called Father. Beside her a small boy materialized, dressed in old clothes from the depression era.

"Ya did good, Mary," the boy said. "Now they can't kill anyone else."

In the kitchen, Alyssa lay face down, motionless, on the floor. A large knife protruded from the back of her neck just below the skull.

Mary turned to look at the boy. "But Arthur, doesn't that make me a killer just like them?"

The boy shook his head. "No, Mary. They were violent assassins. You're just insane," he finished and faded from view.

TWILIGHT

Adam opened his eyes and stared at the shadowed lines formed on the ceiling. His mind automatically attempted to assign mathematical formulas to the patterns. He blinked and sat up. His eyes wandered to the window with the simple vertical blinds parsing the early morning sunlight. He raised his right hand and looked at it. It appeared human.

"Adam?" a woman's voice asked from hidden speakers. "Your counseling session is in fifteen minutes. Do you wish to keep the appointment or reschedule?"

"Keep," Adam said. His hand rose to his throat. It sounded so similar to his normal voice, albeit decades younger. He stood up and walked into the bathroom. A sonic shower, antiseptic basin and a small, handheld sonic cleaning device on the wall were the only things gracing the room.

"Of course," Adam murmured. "Nothing else is needed."

There was a mirror on the wall. More of a video sleeve of polymers that formed the surface of the wall, but it appeared as a mirror when it wasn't serving other functions. He looked at his reflection. A young man in his twenties with blonde hair, perfect features and flawless skin stared back at him. It matched his own appearance thirty years ago with a few embellishments that served vanity more than anything else. As he stared at his reflection, he mused on the pointless nature of the improvements that he'd felt were so important only a few days ago before his transition.

He stepped out of the bathroom and walked to the door of the bedroom. No, not bedroom—home. This room with his bed and the lone bathroom comprised his entire residence now. He paused at the door and looked around. He could see now why that was perfectly adequate.

He left his new residence and journeyed the half-mile to the counseling facility. As he walked, he noted the utilitarian design of the buildings complemented by understated landscaping. The ever rarer trees were nowhere to be found.

He ascended a small flight of stairs and entered the building. His mind retrieved the assigned counseling room number, 17, and he walked to the room. He noticed that he wasn't out of breath from his brisk walk. Then it occurred to him that lungs were no longer required, since the heart and blood in his body were now synthetic. Technically, they were the functional analogs of heart and blood—a tiny fusion reactor and a hydraulic like fluid that allowed for the activation of the various motors and other systems providing locomotion.

He opened the door and looked at the two recliners set up to face a large screen on the wall. He sat in the recliner on the right, glanced back at the door and realized his automatic reflexive checking of the exit was a residual habit that was no longer necessary. The screen lit up and his attention returned to the counseling session.

A woman appeared on the screen. He mused she was nominally attractive, but where there should have been some sort of emotional reaction to this, there was only a mathematical calculation of her features and an appreciation for the symmetry therein.

"Adam," she said. "My name is Valeen. I will be acting as your counselor for your first session. Did you have any problems or concerns relating to your transition?"

"No," he replied. "Everything seems to be in order." He frowned. "Perhaps more mechanical than I expected."

"Perfectly normal. The emotional subroutines and processes will take some time to integrate with your transferred psyche," Valeen said.

"I was told most emotions will return after the stimulation sequences," Adam said.

"That's excellent recall for your first day." Valeen smiled. "That may help with your first visit today."

"Visit?" Adam's artificial synapses fired rapidly. "I don't recall that as part of the induction process."

"Something happened this morning. The FBI has requested your presence." Valeen wasn't smiling. "It's best they give you the details. A transport arrives in ten minutes."

"Is this a new protocol to force emotional growth faster? I'm not sure I'm comfortable with that," Adam frowned again. His synapses were getting the hang of disappointment fairly quickly.

"Standard protocol is weeks of immersion therapy following specific guidelines. There is no new protocol. This was not planned." Valeen looked down. As she did, Adam caught a tear streaming down her face. Intellectually, he knew the appropriate emotional response would be concern. It wasn't occurring naturally yet, but compassion was readily present. He'd always had strength in that emotion and it was easily manifested.

"I'll meet the transport," Adam said.

Valeen nodded.

"There is a change of clothes in the next room," she said, still not looking up. "That's normally for your final counseling session, but the Authority felt it was important for the others to normalize your appearance as much as possible."

She looked up as she wiped a tear from her face. "I'm sorry."

Adam nodded. "Thank you. I'll see you at the next session." Adam smiled.

Valeen smiled back weakly and ended the session. Adam got up and walked to the adjoining room and changed out of his white smock and into a suit similar to the ones he'd worn before transition. He quickly realized he had no direct connection to a news feed and was going into the situation with zero information. Part of that was to aid in a smoother transition—no outside influences unduly affecting integration of psyche and vessel. Clearly, this was a unique situation to pull him out of the transition process so soon.

An automated electric vehicle awaited him at the southern entrance to the facility. He climbed in and took a quick assessment of the interior. A view screen showed advertisements for various items with a small banner running underneath highlighting news items. Stories about continuing research to end the Kaer-Lin virus, global birth council and increasing anti-transhuman violence dominated the headlines.

Adam sat back and thought about relaxing. The physical movement didn't bring the anticipated reaction. Some things didn't translate directly, it seemed. He did a mental diagnostic of his new body. The human reaction of increased heartbeat, dilated pupils and increased adrenaline didn't accompany his mental alarm at the state of the world. It wasn't a surprise that things weren't going well on Earth, but it was disappointing.

The wheels on the vehicle turned out and became rotating lifters as his conveyance first hovered and then rose into the air. The cityscape rolled by them quickly, but not so quick that Adam missed a smoldering crater near and partially consuming the convention center. That was new.

His flight path diverted around the crater. Multiple emergency vehicles were joined by construction equipment to move debris and searchers in the air and on the ground. Adam frowned. The devastation was considerable.

Ten minutes later, the vehicle landed on a helipad next to the local FBI office.

"This doesn't bode well," Adam thought. As the door opened, Adam stepped out and was greeted by a woman in a pantsuit sporting a name tag identifying her as Special Agent Elena Tompkins.

Adam held out his hand. "Special Agent Tompkins, a pleasure to meet you."

"Save it for your brother," she said and turned around walking back to the building.

"Michael," Adam whispered. "What've you done now?" He hurried after Special Agent Tompkins and followed her into the building and to an elevator. They said no more words as the box descended several stories. Adam looked at the indicator above the door and realized they were going to a sub-basement floor.

The doors opened and Special Agent Tompkins walked out, still not speaking. Adam followed and, after two left turns, she stopped and pointed to a door. It was at this moment that Adam noticed the dark circles under her red-rimmed eyes. He nodded wordlessly and opened the door.

Inside the room, an older man dressed in a dark suit stood up. Adam noted the name tag revealed this was Assistant Director Zink Fulgate. Zink held out his hand and Adam shook it.

"Adam, thank you for coming. We're a little at a loss on why he requested you," Zink said.

Adam looked to his left through a large window and saw his brother, Michael, handcuffed to a table. His face was ashen, grey actually, his clothes dirty and his fingers noticeably shook.

"I take it he has something to do with the destruction at the convention center?" Adam said.

"How would you know that?" Zink asked.

"Well, I flew by the site, it seems fresh. He's handcuffed, has a history of protest against transhuman technological advances and appears to be covered in soot from what I'm guessing was some type of explosion," Adam said. "But I confess, I'm shocked he's escalated to this level of violence. Last I heard, he was arrested for throwing a tomato at a legislator."

"Six months ago, Congresswoman Tully," Zink said. "He's been quiet since then until he confessed to knowing about the bombing when he walked into our office this morning. Said he wouldn't say anything more until you arrived."

"What happened at the convention center?" Adam asked.

"Yesterday afternoon, an explosion brought down half the convention center and half the block next to it. We estimate casualties of approximately 1900; we're still putting together the list of the missing. It was a transhuman connection conference," Zink said and shook his head. "We lost several agents assigned to security at the event. With everything that's happening, you'd figure life would be a little more precious, ya know?"

"How can I help?" Adam asked.

"Talk to him," Zink said. "And, by the way, he's not covered in soot. His skin is grey and we don't know why. His clothes were dirty but we can't confirm or deny it's from the explosion. Outside of his confession, we don't have a lot to go on and there could be more bombs. That's our main concern."

Adam took a closer look at Michael and shuddered. At least

the human disgust response was working in his new body.

"He's likely on some kind of life extension regimen," Adam said. "The shaking could be a symptom of the Kaer-Lin virus. You'll need to initiate quarantine and have everyone who has come into contact with him tested and quarantined as well."

"Son of a—Calhoun? You get that?" Zink said.

"On it," a female voice replied through an overhead speaker.

"We should talk as soon as possible," Adam said. "I'm familiar with the theory on what he's doing to stay alive, but I don't know how long it will last. He could be moments away from death."

"Calhoun, hook us up," Zink said.

There was an audible click and then Calhoun responded. "Active."

"Go ahead," Zink said. Michael looked up then, bloodshot eyes revealed some of the strain he carried himself through this ordeal.

"Michael?" Adam said. "It's Adam."

"Well, FBI," Michael replied. "I guess this shell of my brother was the best you could do. He's already left his humanity behind."

Adam turned to Zink and shrugged.

"Well, it's definitely Michael," Adam said. He turned back to the window. "Why did you want to see me? Clearly it wasn't to apologize since our last meeting."

"Our last meeting helped to clear my mind and solidified my mission for God." Michael chuckled and coughed. After he hacked and choked for a minute, he smiled. "Not long now. How do you like my solution to the quick progression of the virus?"

"You always were a brilliant scientist. I assume you ignored the fatal side effects since it wouldn't matter." Adam glanced at Zink, who motioned for him to speed it up.

"Decrease cell production through various means—all cell

production, of course," Michael replied.

"To what end? So you could set off more bombs?" Adam asked.

"No." Michael laughed. "That bombing was merely a calling card to get you out of hiding."

"I wasn't in hiding. Transition takes a month or so," Adam replied.

"Au contraire, my good brother! You're hiding from your humanity. Amazingly, I found an even faster way to strip the humanity from my soul," Michael said.

"Transhumanism is just the next step in evolution."

"It's an abomination!" Michael shouted as he stood up, straining at the handcuffs. Then he started laughing. "But it doesn't matter, God will receive everyone in due time."

Adam looked at Zink who frowned.

"What do you mean?" Zink asked.

"I was talking to the soulless shell of my brother, thank you!" Michael shouted again.

"What do you mean by due time?" Adam asked.

"What's the date?" Michael asked.

"May 27th," Adam responded.

Michael's lips moved as he murmured to himself, "Five days... given time zones... just enough incubation..."

"What?" Adam asked.

"FBI, you do your due diligence on my whereabouts yet?" Michael asked. "Not sure how long I've been here. Passage of time is harder to reckon now."

"It's only been three hours since you arrived," Zink said.

"Doesn't matter, if I die too quickly, you'll figure it all out soon enough," Michael said. He coughed again for a few moments. He spit black phlegm onto the floor and then cleared his throat.

Adam frowned. Without whatever steps he'd taken to extend his life, the virus would've killed him by now.

"So," Adam said. "You've been traveling."

Michael nodded. "Globally," he said. "To maximize exposure."

"Even a single patient zero can only infect so many people," Adam replied. "Those local outbreaks can be quarantined. Still deadly, but hardly planet-wide genocide."

"You would've made a great criminal, Adam." Michael laughed. "But you've assumed the method of transmission was a single organism passing through the communities."

"Even if you had infected partners—" Adam said.

"Do you think I'm an idiot?" Michael shouted. "God gave me this beautiful mind—he gave me the tools to ensure total destruction. One of those tools was Aleet Bendawi."

Adam looked at Zink. Zink shook his head.

"Nigerian born rocket scientist," Calhoun replied over the speakers. "CEO of Worldnet. They had a failed simultaneous launch of 1200 internet drones... two weeks ago. All the drones were lost in the attempt. They, hold on..."

"Exploded," Michael said. "To maximize the seeding of the clouds and the jet stream. Aerosolized contaminant formulated from my own contaminated tissues, designed for maximum dispersal, should've infected everything that breathes by now. Anticipated 99-100% infection and, of course, 100% fatality."

Adam looked at Zink. Even on his fresh transition face, the look of concern was evident.

"Could he do that?" Zink asked.

"Not alone," Adam replied. "But I suspect Aleet was not his only co-conspirator."

"So many people felt the despair introduced by the transhuman threat, they reconnected with God and joined me in our mission," Michael said.

"Extinction level genocide isn't God's plan," Adam replied. "It's madness."

"Oh, now you think you know God?" Michael shouted as black phlegm dripped from his mouth. "God sent this virus to bring his children home before they sacrificed their souls to your hellish transition!"

"What about your much-touted rapture, Michael? Surely you must realize you've thwarted God's plan with your madness. You've proven the Bible is false. No rapture..."

"I've given my people salvation!" Michael shouted again. He clutched his chest and sat down. "They've been *truly* saved."

Michael slumped onto the table and a pool of black liquid flowed from his mouth.

Adam looked at his brother and a tear fell from his eye. He didn't cry for his brother, though; his main concern was humanity.

"Is it true?" Zink asked.

"He was more concerned with being right than saving lives," Adam said. "Have I been any less short-sighted?"

"What do we do?" Calhoun asked, her voice quivering over the intercom.

Adam looked at Zink.

"Contact the CDC. Tell them we suspect an extinction-level event. Give them the details. They'll need to test a sample of people to verify full saturation of the virus among the populace. They'll implement their protocols. The world governments have prepared for this," Adam said and smiled confidently at Zink. Zink breathed a sigh of relief.

"You hear that, Calhoun? Let's get the CDC on the horn!" Zink said and ran from the room.

Adam watched him go. Special Agent Tompkins looked at

Adam from the doorway. She walked into the room and looked through the window at Michael, the black pool of liquid slowly spread around his head.

"So, there's a chance to stop this?" she asked.

"Of course," Adam said. It was a lie, but who was he to take away hope from a race three weeks away from total extinction. Unless his brother was wrong about his projections or the efficacy of his contaminants, humanity had just reached its twilight.

The Most Dangerous Thing

Tendo sat quietly awaiting his master. The eerie purple light visible through the thick windows of the temple cast a dull glow on the granite walls surrounding him. Today was the pinnacle of Tendo's training. Today, he would find out his true purpose in life.

Master Tay-Lis emerged from the temple interior carrying a small book with him. He raised his hand slightly, palm up, and curved his fingers gently, repeatedly. Tendo arose from his seat, his sandaled feet whispered calmly as he walked across the granite tiles. His robes rustled softly with each step. The otherwise silent atmosphere gave reverence to each movement. Tendo bowed when he reached Tay-Lis.

"Tendo," Tay-Lis said. "You've excelled at your teachings. The council has reviewed your birth account, study records and testing. They've found you worthy to take the next step on your journey. Follow me to the Room of Sighs."

Tendo bowed slightly again. He wrinkled his brow as he

followed his master. The Room of Sighs was not documented in anything he had read about the temple. Truly, there were mysteries yet to solve in the world. He glanced out the windows at the rough jagged landscape outside. He wondered briefly if anyone had braved the harsh elements of the exterior world. He smiled grimly. His wondering was foolish. No one had left the inner world for centuries. The Temple of Remembrance was the only part of their civilization that was above ground. Only a select few ever wandered these halls and gazed out among the jagged spires of a dark world.

Plaques lined the walls filled with words of profound wisdom. Tendo's last year has been spent memorizing every line, contemplating every thought of the ancients. Only through reverent observance of past mistakes could one hope to achieve greatness and forgiveness.

They came to a small unmarked door Tendo had passed a thousand times before but had never entered. Master Tay-Lis bowed low before the door and then opened it. Tendo followed his example, bowed low and then joined his master passing through this new portal. They passed by older walls lining a small hallway. The surface of these walls was tougher than the smooth granite surfaces in the rest of the temple. After a time they came to a large, ornate door. Tendo gazed at it in awe. It was made of wood, a material he'd only read about in historicals as a small child.

"How?" Tendo asked and looked at his master.

"The room beyond was created before the Great Calamity when trees were plentiful, or so I've been told," Master Tay-Lis responded, his voice cracked with age. He raised his wrinkled hand to a large metal ring and pulled. The door swung open slowly, creaking on centuries-old hinges. Inside, the familiar natural red glow from the tunnels below lit the interior as it was reflected up small apertures in the floor from below.

The walls were lined with various types of ancient machinery and weapons. As Tendo's eyes passed over each of them, his eyebrows raised with recognition. Arrayed before him were the Forbidden Artifacts—death machinery forged and manufactured by previous generations. He'd only seen these in the texts he studied over the last year.

"The varied array of our civilization's past mistakes," Master Tay-Lis said. "All inoperable, of course. Whenever someone decides a new weapon should be created, we bring them here and show them the statistics for each creation. The magnitude of our own atrocities."

Below each piece of machinery, in addition to statistics about the deaths associated with the device, a rolling video of bodies ruined by the deadly artifacts bared the grisly details. A sea of dead flickered around the room. Tendo's eyes went wide as he gazed at the cautionary images. His eyes eventually fell on a single plain door set in the center of the back wall.

"Is that another exit, master?" he asked.

Master Tay-Lis gazed at the door and sighed.

"Therein lays the greatest weapon of all or, at least, a portion of it," Master Tay-Lis said. "Come and witness the last remnant that brought the worst destruction to the planet."

They walked to the door and opened it. Three walls were solid, but a single thick window let in a purple haze from the outside. On a pedestal in the center of the adjoining small room, a tiny, clear box was illuminated from below and above. Tendo approached the enclosure wide-eyed. Mounted on thick metal posts was a small square of gray material. As Tendo got closer and examined it, he noticed purple lines under the surfaces that moved rhythmically like a heartbeat. He turned to Master Tay-Lis and saw the stony-faced gaze looking back at him.

"What matter of magic is this?" Tendo asked.

"The highest advances of science created the most destructive weapon ever devised. Men who thought they could play God used their knowledge to create an immortal being of unmatched power and ferocity," Master Tay-Lis said. "It was also nigh invulnerable. Only the most cunning of us were able to devise a weapon to bring the beast under control. They had to remove a piece of the creature to disable it."

"It still moves!" Tendo said. He gazed in wonder at the smooth surface, seeming to pulse with life. "Is this magic?"

"No," Master Tay-Lis said and cast his gaze out the window. "Out there, buried under centuries of dust, the rest of the weapon lies, powered by the eternal pulse of a quantum generator revolving with the passage of neutrinos. Never dying, but never at rest—it can't carry on its horrific mission unless it is whole. Those platinum pins hold fast the only bit that has ever been removed from the machine, removed at great expense of life. Regardless, it was finally defeated and will trouble mankind no longer."

Tendo bowed his head in reverence.

"It is your sacred duty to never let this piece be freed. To do so would mean the destruction of us all!" Master Tay-Lis spoke the last with a seriousness and fear he'd never heard before.

They walked from the room and closed the door behind them.

Three weeks later, Master Tay-Lis fell ill and passed shortly thereafter. Rumors passed through the populace about their shrinking population. The birthing vats had failed to produce a healthy fetus in several months. No one seemed to have the technical expertise to troubleshoot the problem; the technology was centuries old and had been failing for years.

An earthquake shook the earth a few months later. The damage was extensive. Many died in a cave-in after the supports holding them up failed; they hadn't been serviced in decades. Fear spread like wildfire as the other supports were examined but couldn't be repaired. The knowledge had been lost to the sands of time.

Tendo had gone directly to the Room of Sighs after the earthquake to look after his responsibilities. The exterior room was intact, nothing amiss. The smaller room at the rear had significant damage to the rear wall. Tendo also noticed a crack in the thick window looking out on the hazardous purple landscape. As he examined the damage to the wall, he noticed pieces of plaster falling from a small hole. He cleared the plaster away and found an ancient manuscript, the brittle pages inside covered with writings. He carefully took the book and moved into the exterior room where he could set it down.

As he moved through the pages, a picture began to emerge. He walked over to a few of the exhibits. One of them had been struck by a falling rock from above. He looked up momentarily, but then returned his attention to the exhibit. The rock had fallen on the plaque underneath. Tendo looked around nervously as he pushed the thin bit of metal aside revealing another underneath. The inscription below told a different story of the weapon of destruction in front of him. Rather than the millions lost, this weapon had never been used. Why had someone changed the inscriptions? Had they changed them all?

He quickly returned to the book. After verifying the changes to several other exhibits, he reached the last pages which described the creation of ultimate salvation. He read through the pages and was horrified by its contents. Could it be true? Did his ancestors destroy it out of greed for power?

Another quake shook the room. Part of the ceiling collapsed near the exit. Tendo sought refuge in the smaller room. This time, the damage had reached here in a more significant way. A chunk of the ceiling had fallen on the pedestal, hitting the enclosure. It had fallen to the ground, cleaved in two. But the thin membrane of skin still held fast, stretched a bit between the broken halves. Tendo jumped back as the top pieces of the enclosure popped and flew up into the air driven by the four metal pins holding the artifact in place. A moment later, the thin membrane of skin rose into the air and shot out of the room through the crack in the window. It happened so fast, all Tendo could do was stand and gape in awe and horror.

Tendo retreated back into the larger room. He attempted to move the debris blocking the exit, but it was too heavy. He was trapped until someone came to check on him. He sat down with his back to the wall and weariness settled on him like a blanket of stone. If the damage had been extensive below, it could be days before they even thought to check on him, maybe even weeks. He had no supplies.

He would die here. With all of the birthing vats inoperable, he wouldn't even be replaced. In all likelihood, he may be the last person alive to see this room. Their civilization was fading as fast as the sunlight faded in the maroon sky.

He must've drifted off to sleep. A huge crash of glass and stone startled him awake. A puff of dust billowed from beneath the door to the smaller chamber. He heard movement, steps in the debris. Something was moved and then dropped. The door creaked open.

Tendo closed his eyes. He just wanted death to come quickly. He didn't want to see the horrible creature open its fangs and devour him.

"This is a pretty disappointing welcoming committee," a voice said. It was a light, melodic sound; so unlike the deep timbres of his people. He opened his eyes a saw a nude woman standing with her head cocked at him. Her skin was the same mottled purple as he'd seen on the patch of skin in the enclosure.

"You're… you're a female!" Tendo exclaimed. He stood up,

pushing his back against the wall. "The danger is real!"

"Still clinging to that theory, I see," she said. She walked up to Tendo. If he could've melted into the wall, he would've. She reached out and touched his clothing. She rubbed it between her fingers. "And still growing clothing in vats? Well, after what you did to the planet, I can see that you don't have many alternatives."

She released his robe and walked around the room. Tendo's ire got the best of him.

"You! You destroyed the surface world!" Tendo pointed a finger at her. As he thought about the words he'd shouted, he quickly put his hand back at his side and trembled. He just accused a god of being dangerous. He took a deep breath and awaited his destruction.

"Well," she said. "Indirectly, I suppose that's true. It certainly wasn't the outcome I wished. When they invited me to the conference center, I had no idea they'd filled the basement with every functioning fusion bomb on the planet. I wouldn't know that had they not bragged about it before setting them off. And then again as wave after wave of them came at my nearly comatose body wielding fusion lasers to cut a patch off my forearm. They died in the thousands from the radiation, but they kept coming. The passage of time was a bit fuzzy, but I think they finally managed it after a year. Aradis must've revealed my single weakness to someone he trusted. Obviously, that proved to be a fatal mistake for so many."

She stopped at one of the exhibits. She pointed at the device on the wall. "You know this actually just prints out flesh for burn victims? Cellular evaporator–that's quite a creative weapon name."

"Why would they do this just to destroy a truth sayer?" Tendo asked.

She turned to him, her eyebrows raised.

"Oh! So you know what I am?" She shook her head. "Didn't think they would've passed that on."

Tendo's shoulders slumped. He pointed at the book on one of the pedestals in the middle of the room.

"I did not find out until that book fell from the wall a few days ago."

She walked over and examined the manuscript, nodding as she perused the pages.

"Well, this at least is primarily true. Amazing. I thought I was the only blasphemous creation of Aradis' design. Didn't know he was also a historian. Well, he was ideologically suicidal."

She walked around the room and pointed at the various items as she spoke.

"Not a brain sifter, but a hairdo styler. Completely unnecessary after the eradication of women, I suppose. And this is a storage cube for information—holds about two hundred years worth of documents, video, audio and scientific data. Not the focusing crystal for a melting laser that killed—" She looked at the plaque. "—three hundred million! Well I suppose if you're going to make up numbers, they might as well be huge."

She continued walking around the room describing the mundane functions of the artifacts as opposed to their weaponized classifications. Every once in awhile, she'd stop and gaze sadly at one of the items noting it had a true plaque description.

Tendo's heart sank as she walked around the room. With few exceptions, she correctly described all as had been noted in the manuscript. A few items had been added after the manuscript had been completed, but she seemed to know what they were as well.

"Women are evil," he said, grasping to the only constant he'd known without doubt. "We learn this from birth."

"No doubt you did. The victors," she said as she pointed at the walls. "Rewrite history as they see fit."

"Did you come to kill us? Have your revenge?"

"Honestly, I was just curious to see what was left of the 'master race,'" she said as she smiled at him. "Not much, I can see."

"We don't need your kind to save us," Tendo said as the hackles rose on his neck.

"You're really not salvageable at this point," she said. "I'd imagine by now, you've lost your technology to history and can't repair or replace the technology you created centuries ago to replace the female womb."

"The what?" Tendo frowned. He'd never heard the term 'womb' before.

"Humanity used to have two sexes, male and female," she said.

"Evil and good. We eliminated the evil." Tendo stuck his chest out, determined to be defiant before his death. They'd eliminated the evil and used their image to purge any remaining evil from themselves as often as needed.

"The history you've been taught is not correct. A sex or even a racial subset of humanity is not inherently evil. Every individual has the capacity for good and evil. Even I, in my arrogance, didn't realize my actions would push those in power to destroy their own world to eliminate me. I'm simply a truth sayer, I'm not infallible. I hadn't learned that sometimes it's better to be silent than speak the truth," she said as she turned towards him. Tendo inhaled sharply as the red glow fully illuminated her bare, alluring form.

"Women and men were two halves of life. When combined, they created life. Babies were not always created in a birthing vat."

As Tendo gazed upon her nakedness, he felt a familiar stirring in his belly. He despaired. He could no longer access the portals of forgiveness where he'd seen her evil form countless times. Evil had appeared to tempt his expulsion to be thrown to the wind.

"You appear in the guise of one who draws the evil from us.

How can you not be evil?"

"Ah, the old teachings—gaze upon evil and extract it from your body. Did you not know they were simply taking your contributions to add to the eggs they'd harvested from the females? They clearly ran out of one half of the equation," she said as she walked slowly towards him.

His pulse quickened. What was she doing to him? He felt the evil impulses rising at his groin. Soon, he would need to expunge it from himself. As she stood naked and peacefully before him, he noticed she had a crevice similar to the portals of forgiveness—there betwixt her legs.

Before he knew what he was doing, he had pushed her down on the ground, released the pressure from his growing evil and plunged it into the portal. She didn't resist, but simply lay there allowing him to complete the ritual.

When he was done, a feeling of peace and calm overtook him. He collapsed on top of her.

She easily rose up, lifting Tendo off of her. She laid him on his back.

"Thank you," she said.

"For what?" Tendo whispered. "I disposed of my evil inside you. Now you will be doomed and destroyed from the inside. I have done what the ancients could not. You will be consumed by evil."

"Because they lied to you, I omitted my other reason for coming back here. I felt you were still healthy and young enough to feel your natural urges. It takes two halves to create life. You've given me the other half. I was created as a truth sayer but also as a woman. Immortality extends to my function as a life-giver as well. Aradis gave me the ability to carry on procreating as long as I had the seed of man available. What you have given will be preserved within me and give rise to millions. But I will wait until this era of mankind has completely perished by its own hand."

She stood up and walked back to the door of the smaller room.

"Sleep now. You may yet live on for a few more years if they come for you."

She closed the door. Tendo heard the movement of footsteps among the debris and then silence. The exhaustion from his effort of expelling evil overtook him. He pondered if the truthsayer had indeed told the truth and then closed his eyes as the tinkle of glass from her final exit echoed throughout the room.

ECHOES

Gallus and Dyntrie entered the small cabin cautiously. Gallus always entered first as his darker hair and complexion gave him a little more stealth than his fair-haired and fair-skinned partner. Though they had been summoned and had every right to enter the building, they'd both been stung enough times by Carlyle's whips and darts to remember caution could save their life one day.

As Gallus' eyes adjusted quickly to the interior, he noted the fire burning in the small cook stove in the corner as well as three lamps burning into the night. Carlyle, a haggard man who always looked a stone's throw from death but surprised the unwary with his strength and flexibility—proved wiry and deadly to opponents who underestimated him. He raised a gnarled finger and beckoned them all the way to the small table he sat behind.

Carlyle eyed the two young men as he sharpened a short diamond-tipped blade on a stone. They nervously looked at each other, wondering if the blade was meant for them.

"I have a mission for you two, both profitable and dangerous," his voice cracked as he spoke. The young men were never sure if this was his real voice or just an act. He set the blade down on the table and pointed at the chairs next to them. "Sit."

Gallus and Dyntrie sat as nonchalantly as they could manage. After six years of training under Carlyle's tutelage, they'd learned to be both alert and cautious. They'd also had it drilled into them to always carry more than one blade and always diamond-tipped. The jeweled requirement was never explained, but they'd chalked it up to Carlyle's eccentricity among his other interesting traits.

"Relax," Carlyle said, his gruff voice sounding lighter than they'd ever heard before. "This is a serious mission. You've completed your training. You'll face death enough when you're in the field."

"If that was supposed to relax us..." Gallus said in his light voice.

"Mission accomplished!" Dyntrie finished, a gleeful smile painted his face.

Carlyle sighed. "That levity may be the only thing that helps you keep your sanity," he said. He pointed at a piece of parchment on the desk.

The thieving duo leaned forward to look at the dark ink marks on the page that created a crude map of a square room. A circle in one corner opposite the door was etched in red.

"The current Baron of Givenchy is rumored to have dispatched a nobleman without the proper authorization. He denies said impropriety, but the rumors persist that he did the deed in his dungeon, well away from prying eyes... or so he believed," Carlyle said as he pointed to the red circle. "This ornamental gem appears identical to the others, but it has a magical property in effect since it's installation during the prior Baron of Givenchy's reign. Alone in the dark, it captures a visual record of all that transpires. Forgotten in the dark corner of what is now a fully functional dungeon."

Gallus and Dyntrie looked at each other and frowned.

"Is this rumored to be in this corner? Who vouches for this tale?" Gallus asked.

"Surely the current Baron is aware of this feature, learned from the last Baron either voluntarily or through other means," Dyntrie finished.

"The previous Baron was unaware as I was the one who installed it without his knowledge," Carlyle said as he thrust the freshly sharpened knife into a cube of cheese and raised it to his mouth.

"You?" Gallus frowned. "Surely you weren't a stonemason in a past life."

"I had a patron of my own who wished for information of an ill nature he could use to overthrow the Baron. Sadly, my patron passed before the gem could be retrieved and so it remained." Carlyle took a draught of wine and smiled. "I was still paid handsomely before my patron passed. I gave it not a thought before I overheard this bit of palace intrigue."

"Who else knows of this? What dangers of discovery will we face?" Dyntrie stood and paced as he spoke. Carlyle grunted as Dyntrie paced, knowing this was his way upon considering a task before him.

"I'm your only liability," Carlyle said. "No one else knows

and I'm covering the reward myself. I'll be gaining other riches beyond justice with the recovery of the gem."

"What is the reward?" Gallus asked from his seat. His style was more relaxed. "More importantly, what danger does the Baron pose to us playing in his domain?"

"One hundred gold each," Carlyle said.

Dyntrie stopped pacing. Gallus sat up. They both looked at each other.

"That's insane," they said in unison.

"The requisite danger is death at the hands of a sadistic Baron who will no doubt torture you for information before skinning you alive... or so the rumor has it for his preferred method of execution." Carlyle stabbed a piece of meat and popped it in his mouth. "From what I understand, he rules by fear. Asking the local populace anything about the Baron would likely lead to your immediate deaths. I obtained that last tidbit from the sole survivor of a band of merchants that chose unwisely to visit the barony four years ago."

"Guards? Defensive structures? Contacts?" Dyntrie asked.

Carlyle chuckled and pointed at the crude map.

"On the east wall, there is a waterfall. The pond at the bottom hides a passage under the water that leads directly to the dungeon. Given your stealth capabilities, I trust you'll be able to slip in and out unnoticed." Carlyle sat back and sighed. "The rest is up to you. Any contacts I had in that barony have long since perished. I haven't been there myself in decades. In truth, I'm not entirely sure the hidden passage is still there, unguarded or otherwise safe to traverse. It is the only information I have on the building other than the gem's location—hence, the rather substantial fee for acquiring the item."

"Why not retrieve it yourself?" Gallus asked.

Carlyle looked down and was silent for a few minutes.

"Hard though it is to admit, I'm not as young as I used to be. I'm certainly spry enough to keep two students on their toes, but I've lost a bit of pep in my step. Combine that with my face being known to several mercenary factions that may be operating in the area and you can see how I'd be in considerable danger before getting anywhere near the Baron's fortress," Carlyle said as he stood up and stretched. "Besides, a wise man acknowledges his own limitations and plans around them - which I have, by your considerable tutelage in the thieving arts."

"Fair enough," Gallus said and turned to Dyntrie. "Satisfied?"

Dyntrie nodded.

"You have your blades?" Carlyle asked as he always did.

"Of course, Master," they replied. Carlyle tossed a small bag to Dyntrie. It clinked when he caught it.

"Good. If the Baron catches you, use them on him or perish. Prisoners don't live long at the barony. That's sixty silver to see to your transportation and lodging costs," Carlyle smiled. "An advance against your reward upon completion of the task."

Gallus shook his head. "Still teaching us the business end of things, I see."

"Would you prefer a lesson in dagger catching?" Carlyle asked.

"No!" Dyntrie said. "We're on our way."

Dyntrie grabbed Gallus by the arm, pulling him up from the chair he lounged in. They left the building quickly.

Three cart trips and several miles hiked on foot later, the duo entered Givenchy. They found the nearest tavern for a drink while they checked out the local populace for any danger signs they might be watched. No one had even inquired as to their business in town, so their carefully concocted stories of a traveling cobbler and stonemason looking for work were never tested. People seemed content to keep to themselves for the most part. The hushed tones everyone spoke in didn't seem to be in reaction to the visitors; it was more like no one wanted to draw attention to themselves. Even the women seemed subdued, dressing plainly to appear less appealing.

"The sooner we leave here, the better," Gallus said. "None of these people really seem alive."

"It would seem the Baron's sadistic tastes weren't exaggerated," Dyntrie said. "We'd do well to follow their lead - keep our heads down and we might survive the next couple of days."

Several ales were consumed before they made their way back out onto the dusty streets and into a fairly modest-looking inn. They shared a room to keep costs down; Carlyle had literally beaten frugality into their heads many times over the last five years. Still, the promise of hot water to soak their aching feet drew them to this particular inn more than anything and the extra cost was worth it. Fortunately, while sore, they didn't sport any blisters from their days on the road.

The innkeeper smiled briefly at them as they paid ahead of time. He looked around the small common room of the inn and then whispered quietly.

"Go out not at night, kind visitors. All who do are left to the Baron's pleasure." He nodded to them both and then took them to their room.

After a small meal at their bedside, they quickly fell into a deep slumber.

The next day found them both refreshed and ready to do some exploring. Givenchy was a medium-sized town with large tracts of well-maintained farmlands surrounding it. High above the town, the towers of a keep could be seen nestled deep in the forest on the mountainside.

"Our quarry, I presume," Gallus said.

"Most likely," Dyntrie replied. "There doesn't appear to be much else that could qualify. Woods seems kind of thick. Hope they didn't divert the water from our anticipated point of entry."

Gallus opened the small backpack he carried. It contained two chisels, small hammers and some rope as well as a bundled set of torches, flint and steel wrapped tight in waxed linen for waterproofing.

"You've got your blades?" Gallus asked. Dyntrie looked at him incredulously.

"Of course! When have I ever not?" Dyntrie shook his head. "You're beginning to sound like Carlyle."

"Good," Gallus replied. "Then we might come out of this alive."

Dyntrie grunted but didn't disagree. He walked into the forest taking his steps carefully to remain as quiet as possible.

After two hours of careful movement, they reached the outer walls of the fortress. Watching from cover, they observed the buttresses for over an hour, but saw no one.

"I don't like it," Dyntrie whispered. "No guards in town and none on the walls. Who protects the Baron? Who enforces the laws?"

"We need to get in and out quickly, before it gets dark," Gallus said. "There's evil afoot. I can feel it in my bones."

They made their way silently to the rear of the fortress where a spring-fed waterfall still flowed from the middle of the keep wall. The pool at the bottom was clear. They watched briefly for guards, but still none appeared.

Stripping off their outer clothing and boots, they strapped the blades back on and secured the backpack. They both dipped under the water and found the opening a few feet below the surface. It couldn't be seen from above; had Carlyle not told them it was there, they never would've known.

They emerged into a small chamber leading to a single passageway, not tall enough to traverse without crouching down. The room was sparsely illuminated by sunlight coming in through cracks in the wall hidden by the waterfall outside. It was just enough to allow them to get out of the water and get their torches out and lit.

Cobwebs lined the single path leading from the chamber; not surprising after decades of abandonment. The ground was slick from dew and moss growing in the dark confines, so they made their way down the descending path carefully. Handholds were naturally present in the walls of the roughly hewn tunnel. Near the end of the passage, the smell of death began to filter in from somewhere in the darkness. Dyntrie held up his hand and Gallus stopped moving.

Dyntrie handed his torch back to his partner and moved to

the end of the passage which ended below an old rusted grate overhead. A small hole underneath led to the sewer system far below.

Dyntrie held his head cocked slightly so he could listen to anything happening in the room above. A small drip of liquid splattered on his neck as he held himself perfectly still, confirming there was no movement or sound in the room. He beckoned Gallus forward with a wave of his hand. Gallus scrambled quietly to him holding both torches.

Gallus gasped. Dyntrie turned to frown at him. Gallus pointed at his own neck. Dyntrie raised his hand to where the liquid had dripped on him. It was a deep crimson. Dyntrie locked eyes with Gallus and took a deep breath. He sniffed in annoyance and pointed to the grate above. Gallus moved one of the torches so it better illuminated the obstacle. Even though heavily rusted, there was nothing but gravity holding the grate in place. Dyntrie pushed it up and stood slowly, holding the metal above his head.

In the dim light coming from below, Dyntrie could see the floor around him was clear enough to set the grate down silently and out of the way. He climbed out of the hole and held a hand down. Gallus passed the two torches up to him. Gallus then joined him in the large dungeon chamber above.

As their eyes adjusted to the light, the room came slowly into focus revealing numerous torture apparatus in the roughly forty by forty-foot room. In addition to large red gems lining the walls about waist high, there were three relatively fresh corpses entangled in the apparatus. It was clear they'd died horrible deaths and fairly recently as the blood still trickled from two of the corpses. Dyntrie stared at the nearest body, a woman of perhaps twenty years of age hideously impaled on spikes. Her arms and legs were strapped to cylinders that had been slowly lowered so the spikes entered her bloodied form at a slow, anguished pace.

Dyntrie jumped as Gallus set his hand on his arm. The room flickered briefly with light from the jostled torches Dyntrie held. Gallus pointed at the door at the far side of the room and then behind them where the gem they sought would be embedded in the wall. Dyntrie nodded and they quickly removed the tools from the backpack and got to work.

The mortar was decades old and fell away easily so they had little trouble removing the gem quietly. So it was with no small surprise that they jumped when they heard a deep voice say "Only a matter of time before he revealed the life stone and sent fresh meat for me to carve."

From beside the closed door, a dark figure seemed to erupt from the shadows and fly toward them, blood red eyes glowing and fingers ending in claws. It was upon Dyntrie before he could move.

Gallus stabbed at the creature with the chisel in his hand, embedding it deep in its throat. It turned its head and laughed at him, spitting blood all over Gallus' chest.

"I'm not a mere mortal, boy!" it shouted. Then it jumped back, screamed and clutched its chest revealing Dyntrie holding his diamond-tipped short sword, black ichor dripping from the blade. Without pause, the duo whipped their throwing daggers into the fleeing monstrosity's back. It exploded in a shower of flesh and fire, rocking the foundation of the fortress and knocking them off their feet.

"Get the gem," Dyntrie said, grabbing at the scratches left

by the creature as it tore through his shirt. The echoes of falling masonry peppered the air above them. "If that wasn't the Baron, you can be sure he knows we're here."

Gallus picked the gem up from where it had fallen and looked at it briefly. It glimmered with an otherworldly light. He tucked it in the backpack without another word and jumped down into the hole. Dyntrie dropped the torches into the passage and followed Gallus, replacing the grate quickly. They scrambled up the passageway bringing the torches with them and extinguished them in the pool at the top of the tunnel.

They slipped quietly into the water and dove down until they reached the opening. They rose to the surface of the pool outside quietly, taking in a breath as hushed as possible. Proving their stealthy credentials, they quickly slipped into the forest and never looked back, only stopping to dress when they'd made it halfway back to the road. Gallus paused as Dyntrie tried to walk by him toward the road. Gallus grabbed his arm. Dyntrie looked back and saw his partner shaking his head. Dyntrie nodded and they resumed their way to the town passing through the forest and avoiding the only road that connected the populace to the fortress.

As they got closer to the town, a large crashing sound shook the forest and an orange light erupted from the direction of the fortress. A loud crack followed by an explosion dropped them onto the forest floor as flames and debris rocketed past them. They quickly got up and ran from Givenchy as fast as their legs could carry them, never looking back.

Days and nights passed wandering the wilderness until they managed to find a trail leading to a small village in the neighboring county. Their training came in handy as they lived off the small game, plants and insects they could find during their trip. Even so, they were parched beyond reason when they got to the town and gratefully accepted their fill of water from the village's well.

Nearly a week passed before they reached Carlyle's cabin. By then, the scratches on Dyntrie's neck had become inflamed and he was feeling weak and feverish. Dyntrie leaned on his partner as Gallus reached to knock on the door. It opened before his knuckles reached the surface. Carlyle appeared in the doorway, reaching out to help Dyntrie into the room. As the stricken thief fell in a heap onto a soft chair, Carlyle looked at Gallus expectantly.

"The Baron or whatever that was scratched him before we killed it," Gallus said.

"The gem," Carlyle said, holding out his hand. After a brief look of shock, Gallus' face became grim. He pulled the gem out of his pack and handed it to Carlyle. Gallus glanced at Dyntrie; the grim look remained on his face.

"I hope it was worth it. I'm not sure Dyntrie will make it," Gallus said. The tone was somewhat accusatory, but he couldn't be too upset. They knew what they'd signed up for—a life or death mission.

"It was," Carlyle said smugly. Dyntrie and Gallus both frowned at him. Carlyle chuckled.

"He'll be fine," Carlyle said as he walked to the hearth.

"It recorded us killing the Baron," Dyntrie said weakly.

"No," Carlyle said as he opened a small jar on the hearth and tossed the contents into the flames. The fire turned blue. "I'm afraid I told you both a bit of a story there.”

“Yeah,” Gallus said. “We guessed that much when he called it a life stone before he tried to kill us.”

“Ahh, it’s a bit more than that. It’s a sophisticated trap, actually,” Carlyle said. “I’m going to have to ask you to trust me again even though I lied a bit about the stone.”

Carlyle pointed at the table behind the duo.

“Your reward and the deed to this small parcel of land are on the table there. It should be enough to set you on to be whatever you want to be after today.”

Gallus looked at the table and then back at Carlyle. “You won’t need it?”

Carlyle shook his head and tossed the gem in the fire. He walked to the men.

“I won’t be here much longer, but I’ll remove the venom and infection from Dyntrie before I go. The least I can do for you boys releasing me from my prison,” Carlyle said. The fireplace popped as the fire cracked the gem and Carlyle slowly morphed into a beautiful angel before their eyes.

The angel reached out to touch Dyntrie’s neck. Blue and green light flowed from the injured man and he sighed. The color returned to his face.

“Fifty years I’ve been trapped here,” the angel said in a lilting golden voice. “Magicks hard to fathom were brought into play. It took decades to unravel the puzzle. Now I can return to reclaim my home after this long exile. Thank you both.”

“But how…” Gallus began.

“Darkness and light are always in eternal conflict, even within each of us. Today you struck a blow for the light.

Tomorrow, who knows? That path is yours to decide. Farewell." The angel rose up through the ceiling leaving the two shocked men staring at the thatched roof above.

"Of all the ways I expected Carlyle to go out," Gallus said as he looked at Dyntrie. "That was not one of them."

Dyntrie grunted and got up. He grabbed the side of the chair to steady himself. "Well, no reason we shouldn't raid his wine stash now, is there?" Dyntrie said and wobbled toward a cabinet in the far corner.

"I suppose there isn't," Gallus said.

ART DEADO

evon pulled up the bank statements again and smiled. His job scouring the business world for vulnerable companies continued to pay enormous dividends. They called him a vampire, called him a vulture, but none of them had amassed over fifty million pounds in just eight short months. Fourteen companies liquidated with ruthless efficiency.

"These Americans," Devon said to his wife Anna as she walked into his home office. "They assume the English are docile. I've been stealing them blind and they're caught flat-footed every time."

"You shouldn't have told Davids," Anna said. "You give him more credit than he deserves."

"We've been friends since childhood," Devon said laughing. "Prime Minister or not, he'll keep our secret. It's the main reason I funded his run."

"He's still a politician," Anna said. "I don't

trust politicians.”

“Money is a primary motivating factor for all politicians. I’m sure his own greed will keep him in line, but seriously, are we any more trustworthy?” Devon said. “I’m certain I’ll never run for office. I enjoy playing in the shadows too much.”

Anna looked out the window. Devon breathed in her captivating beauty. She’d been with him for years, well before any significant accumulation of wealth. How had he been so lucky to capture this dazzling creature in his orbit? She turned back toward him with a kind of sadness in her eyes.

“Is it enough now?” she asked. “Fourteen companies bring a lot of enemies. Surely someone will unravel your web and bring their grievances to our door.”

“I’ve been incredibly careful, Anna.” Devon stood up and grabbed her shoulders encouragingly. “Only our small group of friends is aware of our success and even they don’t know the particulars. It’s an intricate web of fronts and dummy corporations. It would take a genius to follow that trail to a single actor.”

“Devon, you’re a genius, but you’re not alone.” Anna frowned. “There will be others who can pierce that veil.”

“Oh Anna,” Devon chuckled. “I doubt a small time operator like me would come up on anyone’s radar. There are dozens of corporate raiders out there doing this in the open and getting heat for it. I’m confident my activities are lost in the haze and we’re well insulated by distance.”

“Perhaps.” Anna looked down for a moment. When she raised her face again, she was smiling. “You are quite brilliant.”

“That’s my girl!” Devon said, pulling her in for a close

embrace. There was a knock on the office door.

"Hello?" Devon called out.

"Master Devon," Devon's butler, Alex, called from behind the door. "A package has arrived."

Devon went to the door and opened it quickly.

"Cleared?" Devon asked the unshakeable Alex.

"Of course, sir. Scanned and sniffed per your requirements. The dogs…" Alex blinked as he searched for the words. "Didn't alert on the package but did shy away from it after sniffing it."

"Shied away from it?" Devon glanced back at Anna who merely shrugged her shoulders. "Very well, let's see this package that has scared the pooches."

It was a gloomy, overcast day but no rain was forecast. They stepped out in front of the building, but Devon stood at the front door as his security men maneuvered the package on the front lawn. The box was one and a half meters long and nearly a meter wide. It was very thin.

"Who's it from?" Devon called from the front step.

Benjamin Quothers, the security detail lead looked up and walked toward Devon.

"There's no return address. It arrived by post," Benjamin said. "We immediately took It to be scanned. It's only just arrived back. It appears to be a painting."

"Strange," Devon replied.

The men carefully opened one edge and slid the framed landscape painting from the box. As soon as Anna set eyes on it, she shouted at the men.

"Put it back! Bring it inside immediately!" Anna glanced around to ensure no one watched from above.

"Quickly!" Devon added. The men carefully slid the painting back in the box and carried it inside.

Anna pointed to Devon's office and the men carried the box in, leaving it leaning on the sofa against the far wall.

"They are to speak of this to no one," Anna whispered into Devon's ear. Devon raised his eyebrows and then turned to the men including Alex.

"The existence of this package is to be forgotten immediately. Understood?" Devon said.

Benjamin nodded. "With the utmost penalties suffered for non-compliance, we understand."

The other two security men looked at each other in shock and then nodded at Benjamin.

"Your complete confidence is always assured with me, Master Devon," Alex said simply. With that he turned and went somewhere else in the house. The security detail left immediately without appearing to be hurried. Devon shut the door with only himself and Anna alone with the painting.

"What has you so flustered, my love?" Devon said. Anna went to the box and slid the painting out. A large cathedral loomed near the center of the painting with a gallows plainly depicted in front. Two men hung from ropes in mid-execution. A third rope remained empty. Anna bent down to examine the inscription in the lower left hand corner. She stood and whistled.

"This is a lost Van Gogh," Anna said quietly. "Well, I suspect it is. If I'm not mistaken this is an earlier work titled 'The Rope'; it hasn't been seen ever, only described in notes from the original commissioner of the work."

Anna looked at the back of the painting and found a small

piece of paper stapled to the frame. It was modern, having been printed on a laser printer. She glanced at Devon and then crooked her finger at him. He moved next to her and read the note aloud.

"Beauty is in the art of conquest,

Too bad the dead never rest,

After merely one week,

Be careful what you speak,

Stay positive and this is true,

What you care for comes back to you,

Rewards as this are soundly just,

Sinful pride results in dust."

Devon laughed. Anna frowned at him.

"It doesn't seem very friendly," she admonished him.

"I'm certain we are the targets of a rather intricate practical joke," Devon said and patted her on the arm. "You can take what steps you'd like to authenticate this painting, but I'm sure it's just an elaborate fake. Still, I'll have Alex mount it on the wall here in the office. I like the look of it."

"As you wish," Anna said. "If it's really a Van Gogh, it's priceless. Creepy, but priceless."

A week passed and Devon had consumed two more companies, the effects of which were felt well beyond the United States, touching subsidiaries across the globe. Still, Devon was confident in his web of false leads and dead ends the international banking system afforded him. That and he was over ten million pounds richer. Even so, he sat in his office glowering at the computer screen.

After completing his latest liquidation, he'd called Anna

who was out with her girlfriends. She hadn't answered. He'd traced her phone and discovered her whereabouts near a certain hotel known for the confidentiality it showed its visitors. He couldn't be certain, but he suspected his lovely wife was having an affair.

Even brooding of this level can be broken by extraordinary events. As Anna walked in the door, Devon's full attention was occupied by the television. The new Prime Minister, his childhood friend, had called a news conference to announce new business rules to protect businesses small and large throughout the United Kingdom. The steps were meant to counter corporate raiders such as Devon, who seethed with anger.

"How can he?" Devon yelled at the television.

"Oh Devon, what could he possibly do? He's only been in office a week," Anna said, unaware of the Prime Minister's announcement or Devon's suspicions of her activities.

"They've got the majority and with him calling the shots, they'll implement these protections," Devon said, pointing at the television. "That will bring everything into focus for the Americans. Even with their anemic political activity, it's much too great of a chance they'll actually pay attention and implement the same thing. I'll be ruined."

"Ruined?" Anna said. "You're richer than ninety-nine percent of the country and they won't be taking those profits away. Surely, you knew this couldn't last forever, darling."

"Surely, just as I should've known friendships can't last forever. As far as I'm concerned, Keith Davids can take a flying leap off Big Ben." Devon sat down with a huff. "I'll send him a tersely worded conciliatory note on losing his next election. I remember our first combined flogging of another student at the tender age of seven. You'd think shared and previous memories would mean more than they do."

Anna was the first to catch the motion out of the corner of her eye. She looked at the painting on the wall and gasped.

"Devon!" she hissed. Devon's head snapped to look at her and saw her pointing at the painting. He stood up and walked closer to the painting. A figure was walking along the top of Notre Dame. He walked to the edge of the building and jumped off. His body disappeared behind the gallows, but a small trickle of crimson appeared on the painting coming from the location the body would've landed.

"What the hell?" Devon whispered. He frowned at Anna. "That's an unusual coincidence."

"What could it mean?" Anna asked. She touched the painting where the blood flowed but nothing came back on her finger. She displayed her finger to Devon.

"That's a helluva thing," Devon replied.

The television issued a warning bell and a reporter came on looking flushed.

"We've just gotten word," the reporter said, "that Prime Minister Keith Davids has just committed suicide."

Anna and Devon turned their heads slowly to the television, jaws hung open.

"We have unconfirmed reports from several eyewitnesses," the report continued. "The Prime Minister appeared to have leapt from the top of the Palace of Westminster."

The reporter paused, listening to her ear bud. "Specifically, from Big Ben. He arrived to attend a meeting with the House of Lords which was scheduled to begin in just fifteen minutes. We do not have any statements from the government at this time."

Devon walked over and grabbed the remote and shut the television off. He turned to Anna and slapped her across the face.

"This is the poorest joke I've ever had the discourtesy to be a victim of, Anna," Devon seethed with anger. "You'll tell me exactly how you hacked the television signal and rigged the painting."

"I did no such thing!" Anna scowled at Devon. She turned and stormed out of the office.

"I'll find out!" he yelled after her. Devon stepped toward his computer and hesitated. He turned on his heel and walked out of the office. He stormed to the front door, walked through and slammed it shut behind him. He caught a glimpse of Benjamin at the far west perimeter wall to the estate. Devon jumped in his silver Aston Martin DB11 and revved it up. Benjamin walked over and opened the gate. Devon drove up to him at a normal speed.

"I'm going out for a drive," Devon said.

"Of course, sir," Benjamin responded and nodded.

Devon briefly considered verifying the story about the Prime Minister with Benjamin, but decided he may be in on the practical joke as well. He gunned the engine and raced off down the road. Fifteen minutes later, he was in Abingdon, a fairly short drive from Oxfordshire, but far enough to where he felt it was unlikely Anna would have been able to extend her influence to propagate a misinformation campaign.

He pulled up by a random pub and walked in. The telly was tuned into the breaking news story and the customers were buzzing about the suicide. Devon walked up to the bar as he watched the broadcast and ordered a scotch on the rocks. He didn't particularly care about the brand of scotch. He just needed something to numb the impact.

"Shame about the Prime Minister," the barkeep said. "So young."

Devon said nothing but murmured a quick thank you when he got his drink. He took a small swig of the scotch and stared at the reporter droning on.

His thoughts wandered back to his antics with Keith at Cambridge. It brought the briefest glimmer of a smile to his face. He sighed and took another drink. He slapped a twenty pound note on the bar and walked out without finishing his drink. The air outside was thick and oppressive; dark storm clouds threatened the small town. Devon shook his head and climbed back in his car. He took the drive home a bit more leisurely, running through the apology to Anna in his head.

He needn't have bothered. When he arrived at the estate, Anna's Jaguar was nowhere to be seen. He didn't think his mood could get darker, but he surprised himself.

As he walked through the front door, Alex met him and offered to take his coat. He slid the windbreaker off his shoulders and handed it to him.

"Anna?" Devon asked simply.

"She's gone off to see a friend for the night in Cheltenham, sir," Alex replied as he stepped away to hang up Devon's coat.

"Did she say who?" Devon asked.

"No sir. Shall I call her up?"

"No," Devon said. He'd been an ass and it was no surprise

she'd taken a break from him. He walked back into his office and stared at the painting. The blood still moved ever so slightly into an ever larger trickle under the gallows. He walked up to the painting and stared at it closely. The spread of the blood was so organic; he barely registered the spread of it even as he examined it. He lifted the painting down from the wall and turned it over, looking for some mechanics or electronics near the edges. The canvas appeared pure and relatively pristine. It wasn't a pixilated screen.

There was nothing. Even the weight of the painting seemed appropriate for its size. He hung it back on the wall. He stared at the blood for several minutes then stepped over to his computer and sat down. The sudden death of the Prime Minister would have unique effects on the market, effects which his unresolved legislation would never account for. Devon had some research and raiding to set in motion.

The next day, Anna returned with a guest. She still bore a fading red hand print on her left cheek. Devon's eyebrows rose when he saw her guest. It was none other than his barrister, Anthony Balfour. Of course, Devon remembered, Balfour lived in Cheltenham. Is that who she was seeing behind his back?

"Devon, so good to see you!" Anthony said.

"Is it now? Are you here to represent Anna in our little dispute?" Devon asked and portrayed a faint smile.

"Dispute?" Anthony frowned. He looked at Anna. "Oh, I see. No, she hadn't mentioned anything but now I guess I know who reddened her cheek."

"It was a misunderstanding on my part," Devon said. He walked over to Anna and kissed her on the other cheek. "My apologies, my dear. I was distraught at the passing of Keith. It took me completely by surprise."

Anna glanced at the painting and noticed the red blood had changed to a dark brown.

"Did it?" Anna asked. She left the room.

Anthony coughed nervously.

"I, um, was a bit surprised when she showed up on my doorstep last night," Anthony said. "I assumed she was upset about Davids' sudden passing, but then I was perplexed about why she wasn't just here with you. She asked me not to call you and then disappeared into the guest room for the remainder of the night. She didn't even come out for dinner."

Anthony sat on the sofa under the painting.

"I apologize for not calling, Devon. I just didn't see the harm in letting her stay the evening."

"Indeed," Devon replied looking down at his right hand. "Perfectly harmless given the circumstances. Why are you here then?"

"You emailed me last night about the Haslid merger; I drew up the paperwork to put in the bid."

"Of course," Devon walked over to his computer as Anthony opened his ever present briefcase. "Anthony, do you do a lot of busy here in Oxfordshire?"

"I have multiple clients here, Devon. Did you want to retain me explicitly?"

"No, no, nothing like that. I'd soon lose everything I've earned if I indulged in that expense."

They both laughed.

"I was just wondering if you ever had occasion to spend

the night here?" Devon asked as he brought up the figures on the Haslid merger and saw they were indeed within his parameters for a hostile takeover.

"I will confess to spending a night or two here every fortnight when a client meeting runs long and the weather gets particularly fearsome," Anthony replied as he handed the papers to Devon. "Why do you ask?"

"Oh," Devon said looking the paperwork over. "I've got some family coming by and was wondering if you could make a recommendation. They're not close family and I'd rather put them up in a local hotel than have them wandering aimlessly about the estate."

"I typically stay at the Witney, although I don't know that I'd recommend it to impress family." Anthony sat back down on the sofa. "It's one of the more reasonably priced hotels and I'm a bit frugal when it comes to just needing a bed and a hot shower."

"Never have occasion to stay at Malmaison?" Devon asked?

"No, but I hear it's a beautiful property. Lovely breakfast bar, as I'm told." Anthony said. "Are you thinking about expanding into the hospitality industry?"

"No," Devon chuckled. "Just trying to plan for the visit."

Devon looked through the papers and smiled. It occurred to him that putting this document together last night would've taken quite a bit of time and probably dampened any opportunity to do more than say hello to Anna. It was efficient and complete.

"This looks wonderful, Anthony," Devon said. "Thank you for completing it on such short notice."

Anthony stood up and walked over to the desk.

"I'll get the papers in right away. Your broker is actually in town today; I think it's odd he's rarely local," Anthony put the papers in his briefcase and shut it. "But, Devon, you called me to look into Haslid months ago. I just updated the documentation last night. It didn't take but maybe an hour. I appreciate your confidence in my abilities, though!"

Anthony laughed and walked out of the room. Devon heard him conversing briefly with Alex and then heard the front door open and close.

Devon looked over at the painting and smiled.

"Alex, could you fetch Anna for me please?" Devon called out.

"As you wish, sir," Alex replied from the hallway. He listened to Alex walk upstairs and waited.

After roughly ten minutes, Anna appeared in the office doorway. "Yes, Devon?" she said as she walked in and sat on the sofa.

"So, you and Anthony, eh?" Devon said as he stood up and walked to the office door, closing it.

"What?" Anna replied. "No, that's crazy."

"He's aware of the breakfast bar at Malmaison," Devon smirked.

"Doesn't every hotel have a breakfast bar?" Anna replied dully.

"You had a lot of quality time last night with Anthony, didn't you?" Devon accused.

"We didn't do anything of the sort, Devon!" Anna stood up and shouted. "Stop this nonsense at once!"

"As far as I'm concerned, Anthony can blow himself to Bermuda and feed himself to the sharks!" Devon replied and turned around to look at the painting. The phone rang and Devon put it on speaker.

"Devon," Anthony's voice came through loud and clear. "I've got some urgent business in Bermuda. You can check with my assistant on the Haslid paperwork I'm dropping off to the broker right now."

"No!" Anna gasped. "You can't! You—"

"Don't say anything more, Anna." Devon put his hand over her mouth. "Sounds great, Anthony. See you when you get back. Safe travels."

Anna's eyes went wide as they heard the call disconnect. She started to make muffled gagging sounds. Devon let go of her and was horrified to see her mouth and nose were sealed shut with a layer of skin.

"No." Devon stumbled backwards. "I didn't mean…"

Anna's eyes rolled back in her head as her hands dropped from her jaw where she had started to claw at her porcelain skin. She fell to the ground.

"Stop it!" Devon cried out. He turned to the painting. "Let her live! Let her breathe!"

He turned around and saw Anna turning blue. He ran to his desk and rifled through the drawers.

"Alex!" Devon shouted. "Bring a sharp knife quickly and call nine-nine-nine!"

The muffled sound of Alex's feet running through the house gave Devon some hope. He looked at the pen he'd just signed the Haslid paperwork with and then at Anna. With a grimace, he snatched up the pen and ran to her.

Anna had stopped convulsing. Her body was still and her

eyes hung open staring into the abyss. He pressed the pen into the flesh around her mouth, but it refused to penetrate the surface. Behind him, he heard the door open. Footsteps announced Alex had arrived. The audible gasp cemented the butler's grasp of the situation.

"We need to cut her open to breathe!" Devon shouted.

Alex handed him the knife.

"I need to call emergency services, sir," Alex said and left the room for the hallway phone.

Devon gripped the knife in his hand and frowned. He applied the sharp tip to Anna's delicate flesh and tried to carefully cut where he approximated lips would be. Blood oozed slowly from the wound, but didn't pulse or rush out. The smallest amount of pressure remained in her bloodstream without a heartbeat.

Devon dropped the knife and began mouth to mouth resuscitation. He tasted her blood. He saw her chest rise and fall as he blew air into her lungs. He took a break every couple of breaths to give her chest compressions.

When the emergency services arrived, the paramedics took over. The local constable arrived as well. He looked at the blood, the medical team and at Devon, his mouth caked with blood and dripping down onto his chest as he sat and watched them try to revive Anna. They quickly put her on a gurney and wheeled her out of the building.

Devon sat there staring at nothing. On the painting above him, a woman now hung from her neck in one of the gallows' nooses.

Alex walked in.

"Shouldn't Mister Armand be with his wife?" Alex asked.

"I think Devon's done enough. He's going to need to come down to the station with me, I'm afraid," the policeman said. "You should go with Anna, although from what I surmised, she may already be gone."

Alex looked at Devon with genuine concern and then walked away.

"You ready to head out, Devon?" the policeman asked.

Devon looked up, a glimmer of recognition on his face.

"Darren," Devon said to his brother the policeman. "When did you transfer here?"

"Six months ago," Darren said. "I didn't tell you because you're a piece of shit and I never wanted to talk to you again."

"Well, you can eat a bullet, you ungrateful sack of shit," Devon said.

Darren walked around to Devon's desk and began to open the drawers.

"Hey, don't you need a warrant or something?" Devon asked and stood up. His jaw went slack when Darren pulled out the DoubleTap .45ACP Derringer Devon kept for emergencies, placed it in his mouth and pulled the trigger. Two bullets in quick succession ripped through Darren's head. Alex's body fell on the desk, knocking Darren's computer to the floor. It left a spray of brains, skull, hair and blood on the office ceiling.

Tears formed in Devon's eyes.

"Darren?" he whimpered. His baby brother didn't move. Devon collapsed on the sofa.

"I just want to die..." he whispered. He felt his heart beat wildly in his chest. Pain shot up his left arm and he grabbed it, wincing. Through squinted eyes, Devon saw movement in the doorway.

"Darren?" he gasped.

"No," came another voice he recognized. He tried to clear his vision and saw Anthony walking into the room. Alex groaned.

"Why aren't you…?" Devon gasped as he slumped over.

"Dead?" Anthony asked. He walked up to the sofa, reached over Devon and pulled the painting from the wall. "The curse only works on things you care about. Your friend Keith, your wife, although I must say I'm surprised with the way you treated her, and your dear brother, who rightfully didn't think much of you."

Devon grabbed at Anthony's slacks but failed to come back with anything in his fingers. Anthony stepped carefully and set the picture down outside the office. He looked at the changes including a dead policeman at the foot of the gallows and a caricature of Devon in the center of the picture on his knees, grasping his chest with one hand and reaching out with the other. He smiled.

"Just another greedy bastard," Anthony whispered.

Anthony carefully made his way back and kneeled down in front of Devon, looking him in the eyes.

"You see, Devon, I'm immune to the effects of the painting," Anthony said and grabbed Devon's shoulder. "And I have you to thank for it. That quaint little merger you did six months ago before you proffered my services wiped out my father and brother's entire income and retirement. Rather than live destitute on government handouts, they both took their lives. Destroyed," Anthony pulled Devon up to a sitting position and slapped his face as his eyes were beginning to close. "Destroyed, as I said, by their deaths, my mother took her own life and my two sisters, equally devastated by the losses, soon followed."

Anthony stood up. "I told them not to move to America, but they unwisely ignored my council."

Devon gurgled as he tried to breathe.

"So, I hunted this little beauty down and rented it out for a spell to give to you, knowing your greed and avarice would lead you to destroy yourself and everything you loved eventually. I must say, I was surprised you did it inside of two weeks!"

As Devon slumped over, Anthony walked to the office doorway. "Well, burn in hell, Devon Armand; it's truly the only thing I care about at the moment."

Anthony walked through the door, picked up the painting and left Devon to face his sins in the afterlife.

RESURRECTION

arren struggled to open his eyes. He raised his arms to rub his eyes, but they felt like logs. After taking some deep breaths and some furious blinking, the ceiling came into focus. The pockmarked ceiling tiles were pristine. The metal bars between the tiles were dust free. He was somewhere recently constructed.

He struggled to sit up and realized he was on a cot. It smelled new. He pushed the sheet and blanket off and sat up. The room around him was filled with lab equipment. He frowned and rubbed the back of his neck. A circle of hot flesh met his fingertips.

He stood up unsteadily and took another deep breath. Looking around the room, he noticed someone else on a similar cot across the room, a short-haired redhead. A small table at the head of her cot held a set of glasses; he assumed the spectacles were hers.

He looked down and realized his clothes hadn't changed since...was it this morning? He realized he had no way to tell the day or time. He felt in his pocket and found his cell phone was gone, but he still had his wallet.

"Darren," a voice boomed from a speaker overhead. "Nice of you to join the living."

Darren scanned the room for a door. He saw one on the far wall away from the equipment between two large cabinets. He went to it and tried to open it. Scanning the surrounding wall, he noted the security pad. He checked the door's frame. It was metal and fairly solid. The wall around was cinder block; much more difficult to punch a hole through than sheet rock.

"I trust you've found the room adequately secure," the voice said again. Darren frowned. The voice sounded familiar.

"Is that... Eric?" Darren asked.

"Good, your senses are sharp. You'll need that," Eric replied.

"Clearly, If I hope to escape," Darren replied.

"I'm fairly certain you won't," Eric replied and two large screens on the wall opposite the door flared to life. As the screen warmed up and the picture came into focus, Darren recognized two of three people wandering around a plain room. His wife and nine-year-old daughter along with another man he didn't recognize. The man laid down on a cot similar to the one Darren woke up on.

The woman and the child Darren knew very well. His heart skipped a beat and his skin erupted in goose bumps. His wife, Nancy, and daughter, Danielle, were supposed to be in Nantucket with his folks, safe from danger.

"What do you want? I don't have much money, but—"

"Nonsense," Eric replied. "I don't need your money, you know that."

It was true. Eric Banyon was a billionaire industrialist magnate. His wealth was legendary. Kidnapping seemed out of sorts with his public persona. He could literally buy anyone to do anything.

The second screen showed a disheveled and dirty woman shuffling about a room littered with refuse and what appeared to be blood. Darren realized with a shudder that the refuse appeared to be body parts. The woman, Darren realized, was one of the infected.

The rooms on the screen were similar in size and design. A temporary wall sheltered what were likely restroom facilities where his wife and daughter milled about. The other room had no such facilities. The infected had no need for a bathroom, although the verdict was out on how the flesh they consumed was or wasn't voided.

From the rooms similar construction, Darren assumed they were co-located, possibly even in the same building.

"What do you need?" Darren asked as he heard the woman on the cot to his right groan as she struggled to wake up.

"A cure," Eric replied. "The woman on the right screen is my wife."

The redhead sat up and held her head.

"Where am I?" she mumbled.

"Welcome, Doctor Strand!" Eric said.

"That doesn't tell me where I am, and I'm not a doctor," she replied as she pulled on her glasses.

"Your dissertation on infectious diseases is sure to get you that doctorate you're studying for. Quite brilliant! Only a matter of time, really," Eric droned on.

"Great," she said. "You like my work. Why am I..." Doctor Strand's voice trailed off as she looked at the left screen and saw her much older husband laying unconscious on a cot. "Billy..."

"Good, you grasped the stakes of your situation!" Eric said. "The federal government and governments around the world have sucked up all the accredited talent to solve their dilemma, but given their qualms about safety and ethics, I know their efforts will be slow and unreasonable. As the feds refused to use my facility for their infectious disease work, I had facilities available for you to begin. Amanda was infected a few days ago, I suspect the government wasn't pleased with my criticisms and had it done, but I don't have time to enact revenge on those responsible."

"That's Amanda?" Darren said as he walked a little closer to the screen. She was the right height and build from what Darren could recall.

"It is," Eric responded quietly.

"Two weeks before likely irreparable damage to your wife's tissues," Doctor Strand said. "You want a cure in seven to ten days... impossible."

"Seven, to be exact," Eric replied, his voice returning to its detached authoritative tone once more. "At which point I'll release my wife into the room of your loved ones. You'll have a little more time to save your loved ones, but not much. In any case, you won't live to see them again if my wife isn't cured."

"Wait," Darren said. "I'm a molecular biologist that works with plants. I'm not exactly perfect for this work."

"Doctor Strand will need a capable lab assistant and the cure will need a reliable method for spreading through the infected's body. You did undergraduate work on nanotechnology, correct?" Eric said perfectly matter-of-factly, not as if he was a maniacal madman.

"Correct," Darren sighed. "So we were literally the best you could find."

"Had to think outside the box in a very short amount of time," Eric replied. "Your facility is underground. There are a few other rooms with supplies and every type of equipment you could possibly want for the task at hand. You cannot escape the facility without wasting precious time. Your loved ones are not here, but rather states away in another hidden location. Don't think I won't hesitate to release my wife earlier to meet your loved ones if I determine your efforts are toward anything but finding a cure."

Darren looked at Doctor Strand.

"Well, Doctor, are you ready to get started," Darren said. Doctor Strand nodded and walked over to the computers arrayed between cabinets with supplies. She paused and stepped over to a refrigerator and opened it, examining the contents. She straightened up and looked at Darren.

"We appear to be well supplied with samples and Petri dishes," she said as she walked over to the computer. The screen came on as soon as she touched the mouse. "No password—this is an isolated network? I see we've got plenty of industry standard software to work with."

Doctor Strand sat down and began moving through the file system. She nodded at certain times and then rummaged around for a paper and pencil to jot down some notes.

"Darren's your name, right? Or was I dreaming?" she said. Darren chuckled and nodded. She handed him the notes she had jotted down. "See if you can find these supplies in the cabinets or wherever."

"You got it," Darren said. He grabbed the notes and moved to the nearest cabinet. He opened the door, blocking the view of all the cameras. He glanced down at the paper as he pretended to search the cabinet. The note read:

Sodium chloride - we don't have time

Potassium chloride - to waste getting out

Syringes - of here before our host

Pipettes - uncovers our connection

Beakers - find a way out

Watch glass - he's solved our other problems

Darren smiled as he pulled several containers and other supply items and brought them to a table. Doctor Strand got up and walked to him.

"You found everything okay?" she asked.

"Not a problem," he said. "There are some other rooms with more supplies. I'll check them out so I know where to go for what we need."

They locked eyes for just a moment of understanding and then Darren walked to the door. He reached for the handle and found it unlocked this time.

Darren entered the exterior hallway and saw it ended at an elevator. He looked around and saw several doors which he assumed went to supply rooms. He scanned the ceiling as he went into each room, searching for any possible avenues of egress like a ventilation conduit or a maintenance hatch. He saw the ventilation grills on the wall which surely led to the other rooms, but it would be a gamble to discover a way out without some kind of map.

He made busy looking for the supplies on the list, hoping their malevolent benefactor would get peace of mind seeing them being proactive toward a solution. In reality, he'd done Jenna and him a favor. Their illicit affair had been going on for over a year now and extricating themselves from their existing commitments had been worrisome. This billionaire bozo was essentially killing off the problem for them.

As Darren returned with an armful of supplies, he glanced around the hallways nonchalantly. Acoustic tiles in here just like all the rooms. They could be hiding additional egress points. He'd have to depend on Jenna's computer expertise to do something about the security cameras. He wasn't sure what Eric had in mind if they tried to escape, but it was clear he didn't value human life. That made him almost as dangerous as Darren and Jenna. Two sociopaths just wanting each other, no strings attached. Maybe three sociopaths doesn't make a crowd, it makes a solution.

He walked back into the large laboratory room and Jenna looked over at him, giving him a brief smile of acknowledgement. Darren set the supplies down on a table. He walked over to Jenna.

"How's it looking, Doctor Strand?" he said.

"Not as dire as I first thought," she replied. "It looks like we've got some real possibilities for progress."

Darren translated her words into a positive assessment for the computer security. She could break it and the network wasn't isolated to just these rooms, but to the entire facility.

"Best we get this going as fast as possible, just in case our first attempts aren't successful. We may need several tries." Darren's words, like Jenna's, had double meaning. When the zombie infection first erupted six months ago, they'd discussed taking advantage of it to eliminate their respective families. As he examined the furniture and equipment for possible exercise in escaping the facility, he had to use all his willpower to keep from grinning ear to ear at his good fortune.

The pair convinced the billionaire to send down some additional equipment. It gave Darren and Jenna the brief access to the elevator they needed to access their most likely escape route. While Jenna ran medical trials with new findings, she also managed to punch through to data on the elevator model and discovered it had a pulley system, meaning they'd have access to cables once they breached the maintenance hatch at the top of the elevator cab.

As they made their progress toward escape, Darren was troubled by Eric Banyon's behavior. He'd known Eric through Nancy. Eric was a longtime family friend and godfather to Danielle. While the married couple hadn't been particularly close to Eric after the marriage, Nancy still considered him a close family friend.

He guessed grief could really change a person. He was glad he'd never have to find out.

Two days passed as the duo witnessed Eric Banyon's wife devour two human beings and noticed the pause in her behavior when she had consumed the human liver. Jenna noted the behavior and included that track of inquiry into her search even as she broke into the buildings surveillance system and made copies of their recorded time in the facility. They'd need that for playback later as cover for their escape.

On the third day, Darren wolfed down another batch of ramen noodles and dehydrated vegetables, when Jenna sat down with him.

"Ready for this to be our last meal here?" Jenna said quietly.

Darren nodded as he shoved a spoonful of noodles into his mouth. He munched on them thoughtfully.

"Eat up," he replied. "You'll need your strength."

Jenna's eyebrows rose mischievously and Darren could feel his pulse pound in his temples with his excitement. The brief flirtation was nearly enough to send him over the edge after being in such close proximity to his lover, but not being able to show her any affection.

They ate the meal quickly and then Jenna walked back over to the computer and typed for a moment in the keyboard.

"There," she said. "Video loop is running and the live camera feed has been turned off."

Darren walked up to Jenna and pulled her into his arms, smashing his mouth against hers in a passionate session of sucking face. They kissed for several minutes and Darren's hands began to roam, groping and clutching his lover. She returned the attention at first, but then pushed him back.

"I think we'd better save that for later." Jenna smiled as she put a finger to Darren's lips to stop his objections. "We don't know how far we'll need to travel."

"I understand although parts of my body are demanding immediate satisfaction," Darren said pointing to the rising bulge in his trousers.

"Later, tiger."

They went to the food supply and quickly packed food and water for a trip. They had to balance what they could carry with what they knew they could probably scavenge from the wild if it came to that. Darren assembled a duffle bag of sorts to carry tools and items to pry doors open on their escape route. Finally, they moved to the elevator. Darren pried the security plate off with a screwdriver and reconnected the wires to open the elevator shaft door. Luckily, the cab was still there from the previous trip. As they stepped inside, Jenna paused and grabbed his arm gently.

"Darren, there's something we need to discuss," she said.

Darren's eyebrows rose as he waited for her to continue.

"The liver enzymes. They are the path to a cure. I found some research data from a French team and they were going down the right path before that facility was overrun. If we went back in there and worked for another day or two, I'd have the cure."

Darren considered it for a moment. He looked at her and smiled.

"Then we can get richer than that pathetic excuse for a billionaire Eric after we get out and deliver that cure in a couple of weeks, once our little problems have been irreparably infected."

Jenna smiled back and they resumed their escape up through the elevator shaft. Using a series of clips and stops he'd banged together, Darren got both of them up to the top of the three story shaft. He pried the doors open at the top and the two stepped out into the open.

They looked around them at a twenty foot high concrete wall

that completely encircled them. Three sets of large steel doors dotted the wall. High up on the wall, a stadium sized display showed a live video shot of them both standing there gaping.

"I thought you said we were free and clear," Darren whispered angrily.

"This was supposed to be enclosed by a chain link fence," Jenna hissed back.

Eric Banyon's face popped up onto the screen. He frowned at them.

"You're going to let Amanda die, Darren? We'd broken bread together in Cape Cod, for chrissakes!"

"Eric, it's nothing personal. But you kidnapped us! What were we supposed to do, rationally?"

Eric laughed. Jenna and Darren looked at each other and the concern really began to sink in.

"There's nothing rational about your affair and your plans to kill your families, is there Darren and Jenna?"

"Uh, look. We can go back down there and get that cure done for your wife. It's maybe two days away at most," Jenna said.

"Well, Doctor Strand, now that you mention it, you were on the right track with the liver enzymes," Eric said.

"How did you—" Jenna began.

A recording of them in the elevator showed their entire conversation taken from a hidden camera. After that, a spliced version of their conversation after Jenna had supposedly shut off the video cameras in the lab revealed both their conversation and their intimacy.

Behind them, the doors Darren had pried open shut and the entire top floor of the shaft began to sink into the ground.

"Ah, hell," Darren said. He ran around the perimeter, looking at the steel doors for a way of getting out. He considered using the hinges as steps to propel them toward the top of the wall. It was a long shot, but he was quickly running out of options.

"But please," Eric continued. "Don't worry about Amanda. She's fine." He turned away and shouted off the screen. "Come say hello, Amanda!"

After a few moments, Amanda appeared on the screen next to Eric. She waved and smiled.

"What the hell?" Darren said.

"A little Hollywood makeup and trickery, my good, good friend Darren," Eric said. Amanda walked away and he returned to viewing them from the center of the screen. "Same with your loved ones. Once I'd shown them proof of your infidelities, they were more than happy to submit to three days of filming while you two were banging away in LA."

The screen switched again to show Nancy and Danielle slightly further away from the camera, waving at them.

"Just your two little problems here, Darren!" Nancy shouted. Then both mother and daughter flipped Darren the bird. The screen then switched to Billy, who stared disapprovingly at them.

"You deserve what's coming, bitch," Billy said. He then stood up and walked off camera.

"What's coming?" Jenna whispered.

"You'll both be tickled to find out the cure was found yesterday and, though the world governments are in shambles at this point, there's a solid effort at mass producing a vaccine. No one knows what the world will look like afterwards, but there's a shining horizon for those of us that survive."

"What's coming?" Jenna repeated louder.

In response, the screen showed news reports of zombies overrunning various cities and secured facilities like the one Jenna worked in at Berkeley and Darren's hometown in San Jose among many others. Additional footage showed military with flame throwers surrounding the infected areas and lighting everything on fire.

"You were both removed from these areas roughly two days before they were overrun. According to unofficial government records, you're both among the dead. Which is very fitting, I suppose."

"Hey!" Darren shouted. "We're not dead! You need to let us go!"

"What's coming?!" Jenna screamed.

"To combat spread of the infection, the terminally infected are being burned. I was able to procure a few specimens before certain populations were decimated," Eric said, his face devoid of emotion. The steel doors started to creak open. As the seals on the doors broke, the sounds of groans and murmurs rose in the compound. The dead walked.

Darren peered into the sealed areas as the dead started to flood out.

"I'm sure there are doors in there somewhere we can breach," Darren said grabbing Jenna's hand.

"It took me three months to erect this facility and put everything into place. Thank you for keeping those efforts from being in vain. Also, good luck breaching the vault doors that lead to the outside before you're ripped to shreds. Good karma to you both!"

TALISMAN

"It's not on him," Alejandro said.

Maravich flipped her black trench coat over the back of the chair as she sat down at the dining room table looking down at the body of Hal 'Chitti' Garrison. A pool of blood had formed below the man's head. He was still face down, a matted circle of brain matter, hair and blood prominent on the rear of his skull. Maravich rubbed her chin and frowned, her dark skin glistening in the heat of the day.

She snapped her fingers and three more people entered, all dressed in the haphazard rough fashion of recovered clothing typical of wasteland marauders.

"Flip him over," Maravich said. Alejandro complied, aided by his three fellow Marauder Krew members. In the center of Hal's forehead, a neat bullet hole was surrounded by a small circle of blood trailing down his nose.

Maravich leaned over and examined the bullet hole. She turned to Alejandro.

"You?" Maravich asked.

"Yes," Alejandro replied and then added, "He was pulling a gun."

Maravich nodded and smiled. She turned to the other Krew members and pointed at the head wound.

"Excellent marksmanship!"

The Krew murmured their agreement. Danya, the tall albino woman, sneered. Maravich raised her eyebrows and stood up. She walked to the other Krew members and examined their faces. Danya was just as tall as Maravich.

"Gun," Maravich said simply and held her gloved hand out to Alejandro. He swallowed hard and pulled his handgun from his waistband behind him. He handed it to her.

She examined the weapon. She looked back up at the three Marauder Krew members and frowned.

"Can any of you do that from ten paces away?" She scowled at the three. The two male members looked down, but Danya met her gaze.

"I could," she said defiantly. Maravich held her eyes, nodded and turned back to Alejandro.

"Well, Alejandro, if the talisman is not on Chitti, ask him where it is," Maravich said as she sat back down.

Alejandro looked down at the corpse and frowned. He looked up at Maravich like she was crazy.

"But he's dead..."

"Ask him," Maravich said and set the gun on the table in front of her. Alejandro swallowed hard as he saw Maravich clench her teeth, the muscles along her jaw line rippling slightly. The steely look in her eyes instantly brought beads of sweat to his brow.

He nudged the corpse with his foot.

"Hey, where's the talisman?" Alejandro said and giggled nervously. They all waited and, of course, the dead man remained silent.

"Maybe he couldn't hear you," Maravich prodded. "Louder."

Alejandro glanced nervously at Maravich. His eyes wandered to his Marauder Krew who all watched him impassively with the exception of Danya who glared disapprovingly.

Alejandro got on his knees next to the corpse.

"Where is the talisman?!" he shouted.

Sweat dropped from Alejandro's brow as he stared at the man he'd killed a mere fifteen minutes ago.

"Maybe," Maravich said quietly. Alejandro's head shot up and he looked at her. "He doesn't know what the talisman looks like. Describe it to him. I'm sure that will loosen his tongue."

Alejandro blinked and tears formed in his eyes.

"Please, señora, he is dead."

"Do. It." The words were spoken firmly, slowly and distinctly.

Alejandro looked down at the body.

"The talisman we're looking for is about six inches long with a blue stone at the top-"

"Aquamarine," Maravich interrupted.

"Que?" Alejandro replied automatically, not able to process the request fast enough to realize the futility of his question.

"Chitti might misunderstand, thinking its topaz or even sapphire. If he's confused, do you really think he can give you a proper answer?" Maravich smiled thinly at Alejandro.

"The blue stone at the top is aquamarine. The rest of the talisman is like a cross with a loop at the top."

"It's called an ankh, Alejandro."

Alejandro's lips quivered as he stared at the corpse. A fly landed on the dead man's face.

"The shape of the talisman is an ankh," Alejandro finished. His hands hung at his side in defeat.

There was a long silence.

"So, Krew, what have we learned today?" Maravich asked,

turning to view the others.

"Don't kill the person you're going to interrogate," Danya answered.

"Exactly right," Maravich said and stood up walking to her. "Now, I'm going to put you to the test, Danya."

Maravich ejected the clip from Alejandro's gun and set the gun back on the table.

"Alejandro, take your gun so we can properly train Danya on apprehension techniques."

Alejandro didn't move.

"Alejandro, don't tell me you wish to shirk their training!" Maravich said holding her fingers to her lips in shock.

Alejandro still didn't move. Maravich walked away from the table and stood in the far corner opposite the door.

"Take. The. Gun."

Alejandro reached up with a shaky hand and grabbed the gun. He wiped the sweat from his brow with his other hand and absently tugged on his shoulder length black locks.

"Danya, out and back in. Get the talisman from Alejandro," Maravich said. Danya stepped out the door, stepped back in and shot Alejandro in the right shoulder. Alejandro screamed in pain, dropped the gun in his right hand and grabbed his shoulder.

"No," Maravich said. "That was luck in disarming him. Always shoot for the hand… try again."

"What?!" Alejandro screamed. "I'm already shot!"

Maravich walked over and picked up the gun.

"Good point." Maravich manipulated the gun briefly and inserted a single bullet. "It will be more realistic if you have live ammunition involved."

Maravich handed the gun back to Alejandro, who tried at first to grasp the gun with his right hand but then realized he couldn't raise his right arm. Danya squinted her eyes at him and then walked out the door. Alejandro sheepishly took the weapon in his left hand. He raised it and pointed it at the door. Maravich resumed her position in the corner.

Danya entered the room. Alejandro squeezed the trigger and nothing happened. He looked at the weapon in horror.

"The safety!" he shouted as Danya raised her pistol and shot him square in the left hand, knocking the gun from his grasp. He ducked down in pain at the additional bullet wound.

"Ahhh! Please stop!"

Danya stepped forward to the edge of the sturdy wooden table Alejandro huddled behind.

"Where is the talisman, Alejandro?" Danya said sweetly.

"I don't know!"

Danya stepped around the table, pointed her weapon and shot Alejandro in the left leg. Alejandro howled in pain. He scrambled back toward the corner.

"It's shaped like an ankh with an aquamarine stone in the loop at the top," Danya said calmly. "Are you sure you haven't seen it?"

"It wasn't on him!" Alejandro yelled in desperation. Danya fired another bullet into Alejandro, this time his right leg. Blood began to trickle beneath Alejandro as it pumped from his wounds.

"Where is it?" Danya shouted. Without thinking about it, Alejandro's eyes involuntarily edged up to the ceiling. Maravich looked up and smiled. Visible in the light fixture on the ceiling was a small ankh shaped shadow.

"You see, Alejandro," Maravich said as she climbed on top of the table and retrieved the talisman from the light fixture with her gloved hand. "A properly rendered interrogation can reveal the most interesting information. I wonder if you wanted to keep it from our benefactor out of concern for your fellow man or were just greedy and thought you could fence it for more than you were paid."

Maravich walked to the door and turned to smile.

"Danya, he's earned his reward."

"No, please!" Alejandro reached toward Maravich but she'd already turned her back. Danya fired once into Alejandro's abdomen. He clutched at the wound with his hands. He sobbed, tears in his eyes as he looked up at Danya, his eyes pleading for mercy.

"You're a traitor, Alejandro," Danya said as the other two Krew members watched in morbid fascination. Danya briefly ceased her torture to put additional bullets in her weapon. "Traitors don't get mercy."

Maravich stood outside the building and listened to the slow additional gunshots and the screaming from the former leader of the Marauder Krew. The entire procedure took about fifteen agonizing minutes. Her smile grew a little broader with each gun shot. Danya would make a fine replacement for Alejandro.

As Lieutenant Olivia Peña entered the warehouse, she could hear the clicking of the camera in the small internal office as the technicians took pictures of the crime scene. Observing the technicians from the door, Detective Vincent Green turned his head at the sound of her approaching footsteps. Olivia raised her eyebrows and Vincent smiled, ruffling his ginger mustache.

"Good to see you back, Lieutenant," Vincent said. "Sorry to welcome you back with a bloodbath."

"Gang related?" Olivia said as she poked her head in the room.

"Of a sort," Vincent replied. "Looks like a Marauder Krew execution. Fifteen bullets. Final one through the roof of the mouth as the vic opened it to allow the barrel in."

"They haven't been active for over five years," Olivia replied. "I heard their leader died."

"Maybe he's just been lying low," Vincent replied. "Or maybe they got a new leader."

Olivia shook her head.

"A violent cult like the New Millennium doesn't switch leaders midstream, or ever really," Olivia said as the technicians walked out of the room.

"We got it all including a partial boot print on the desk in the blood. Got samples of the splatter too," the lead technician said. "It's all yours. I'll have a tech standby in case you find anything of further significance."

Vincent and Olivia stepped carefully into the room. They looked casually around the room before settling their eyes on the bodies.

"Second vic is Hal Garrison, Age 34," Vincent said.

"Chitti…" Olivia whispered.

"Yeah, he has gone by that nickname in the past. Has a rap sheet for moving contraband and fencing just about anything. No crimes for the last…" Vincent scrolled up the pad. "Five years."

"So, Chitti had something that New Millennium wanted," Olivia said. "Maybe he's had it for the last five years."

"You think that's why they went silent?" Vincent asked.

"Lord knows it was a relief when they did." Olivia shuddered. New Millennium had been one of the most violent cults in history, actively slaughtering enemies and anyone it didn't agree with. Over a ten year span, Olivia was aware of at least 300 people they suspected were killed by cult members. Nothing they could pin on the reclusive leader, of course. FBI had helped them catch several of the more violent members, but they'd never been able to catch the infamous Marauder Krew as they called themselves.

"The other vic looks familiar," Olivia said.

"Haven't IDed him yet," Vincent said.

Olivia's eyebrows went up. "I'll be damned; I think that's Alejandro Gonzalez!"

"Who?" Vincent typed the name into his pad.

"When I was working the New Millennium cases, his name came up several times. I think he was the leader of the Marauder Krew." Olivia walked around to the feet of the two victims. "Chitti has a single gunshot to the head. He wasn't interrogated Marauder Krew style. But Alejandro has the classic wound pattern of a Krew torture and interrogation. Also, he's dead, so they must've found what they were looking for."

Olivia watched where she stepped, but got closer to the table. She looked from the bloody partial boot print to the ceiling and saw the lamp fixture.

"Get the techs in here to pull down this lamp fixture carefully. We need to find out what was hidden inside it if we can. Preserve the dust pattern," Olivia said. Vincent ducked his head out the door and barked instructions.

Olivia didn't need pictures to put it all together. Chitti was the designated keeper of the Talisman. The Darkside Collective had arranged that years ago along with a shield from prosecution for the crimes on his rather lengthy rap sheet. She needed to talk to Otto immediately.

"Vincent," she said. "Get details on the old Marauder Krew. It's possible some or all of them have resurfaced. I'm going to shake some trees on the New Millennium beat and see what falls out."

"Going to hunt down the Marauder Krew for this?"

"No," Olivia said. "We're going to try to prevent a war."

Olivia strolled along the cobblestone street until she reached a stairway leading down. Even though she'd been watching for a tail the entire time, she still made a casual check for any observers. The streets were filled with not much more than tourists at this hour, basking in the sunlight, hiking the hills of the city. Even so, her senses told her she'd been followed but she couldn't see who. It couldn't wait until she was sure. Lives hung in the balance. She descended the stairs.

The outer door was a simple wooden one with a small video camera. The door looked flimsy, but that was a deceptive camouflage. Olivia knew it would take a fairly large explosion to strip away the reinforced outer door to reveal the inner steel vault door. These precautions were all designed to slow down the enemy, allowing escape through various other routes. Nothing would stop a determined cult member. It was something they hadn't needed to worry about for five years.

The lock clicked as the door keeper recognized her and she pulled the thick panel open. What couldn't be seen through the darkened, frosted bulletproof windows on the outer door was the vault door located ten paces into the building. The walls were triple cinderblock, packed with Kevlar lining between each layer and shielding another layer of thick reinforced steel wall. The doors were the weak points.

She glanced behind her out of habit, just to make sure she wasn't watched by anyone who shouldn't see what she would do next. She grabbed the thick brass arms of the wheel and turned it until the one with the infinity symbol etched into it pointed to two o'clock. She stepped to the right and looked into the camera which verified her retinal details. There was a small audible beep sound and she grasped the wheel again and pulled the large door open, revealing what looked like a long hallway lined with safety deposit boxes. Even at this stage, it was still designed to look like a vault for regular valuables should someone not knowledgeable about its true purpose try to breach it.

She walked in and waited for the huge door behind her to shut on its own. When it shut with an audible thud, she walked forward and took the branch to the left, walking into the small alcove of safety deposit boxes. On the right wall, three in from the back wall and six down, she spun the combination lock on the box and a fake floor slid open behind her revealing a simple set of concrete steps leading down. She smiled as she remembered sabotaging the drilling machine for the new traffic tunnel so they could relocate this underground facility well away from prying eyes, filling in the old facility with simulated bedrock.

After descending three flights of stairs, she came to the elevator; the last physical line of defense before reaching her final destination. Anyone entering the elevator would be gassed when the doors closed. Perchance they had protection against that, the elevator led down a shaft to a set of rooms filled with valuable items worth a king's ransom. All of it was a decoy.

She pressed her hand to the wall to the right of the elevator doors about two feet up and two feet from the corner, a place where no one would likely accidentally press their hand were they to get this far. The wall slid back revealing a small alcove to the right which she quickly stepped through. As she stood in the alcove, the hidden wall opening slid back into place, revealing another lobby with another set of elevator doors. She walked to them and they opened automatically. She stepped inside, the doors shut behind her and the elevator began its ten minute descent. Even she didn't know exactly how far down it went, although she had estimated it was nearly a mile down. Her ears adjusted to the pressure halfway through the ride.

The doors opened to reveal a simple corridor with offices lining it. Windows on each wall were clear, but could switch to opaque within a millisecond under threat conditions. She walked through the complex until she reached a non-descript door several turns in and opened the door revealing a cozy foyer one would typically see in a small mansion. From here on in, the living quarters were nearly identical to a residence above ground with the absence of windows in favor of changeable screens revealing various pastoral scenes. She ascended the grand staircase on the right side and took a right at the top of the stairs. Two doors down, she knocked.

"Enter!" shouted an old woman's voice. Olivia opened the door revealing a luxurious study, with walls lined by hundreds of books. In an easy chair under a lamp sat an old woman dressed in a brown flannel shirt and blue coveralls. She looked up at Olivia and smiled, her dark eyes twinkling in the light.

"Olivia, nice of you to visit. Although it's not the typical annual check-in, so I must assume you bring interesting news of some sort," the old lady frowned.

"Dara, I'm sorry I haven't been by frequently, but you know I have to do my job top side to maintain our cover and intel," Olivia said as she walked over and sat in the open chair to the old lady's left.

"Sure, always too busy to visit the elderly." Dara waved a hand dismissively and went back to examining the book in front of her that Olivia could see was filled with Egyptian hieroglyphics.

"Marconi is active again. I have reason to believe his forces have retrieved the talisman," Olivia said. "You told me if he recovered the talisman again, the dark would rise and consume the world."

Dara huffed and turned a page. She resumed her study of the hieroglyphics.

"What do we do?" Olivia said, irritation rising in her voice. "This is clearly an emergency, we need to marshal the forces, retrieve the talisman and beat Marconi back to the Stone Age."

"You didn't listen well," Dara replied absently, her fingers tracing the symbols in front of her. "I said the dark would bring the light to balance out the world. We have but to wait for the light to emerge and defeat the darkness."

"Without the talisman, Marconi killed hundreds just a few years ago. With the talisman, he could kill thousands. We can't just wait for some 'light' to emerge. We need to act now, before it's too late."

"Millions," Dara said. "Honestly, if you underestimate the power of the talisman in Marconi's hands, I don't know what I'm going to do with you. Have you forgotten your studies so soon?"

"Dara, we have all of this built, all these forces at the ready to combat dangers just like this. We have to put them on alert."

Dara stopped what she was doing and fixed Olivia with a kind look.

"Olivia," she said. "These forces will be deployed when the time is right, when the light has been triumphant. Until the light rises to meet the dark, it would be like throwing mud at a castle. Completely ineffectual."

"Marconi is dangerous. He has to be stopped. If you're not going to bring the forces of Darkside together, I'm just going to have to try to stop them myself. I hope you'll reconsider and take this seriously."

Dara hummed and returned her attention to the book.

"Thank you for stopping by. Could you bring some scones from The Crumpet Shop next time? I've always found them to be just the right balance for my chamomile tea."

Olivia stood and grumbled. She walked to the door and turned back. Dara kept on reading her book, paying Olivia little heed. The hotheaded lieutenant mulled over the referenced lessons for a moment, then walked through the door and shut it behind her firmly.

Inside the study, Dara looked up from her book and smiled.

"And so the light rises..." she said and looked back down at her book.

THE DARKEST DISCOVERY

The wide open expanse of the hilly tundra soothed Alan Jeffries' soul. The crisp blue skies brought cleansing thoughts to his mind. The loneliness of living so far from civilization was a small price to pay for the safety of the world at large. This was where his darkest impulses could find no purchase—alone at the end of the earth. So it was with no small amount of displeasure that Alan greeted his first visitor in ten years.

Doctor Brenda Higgins walked the two and a half miles from the air strip through the sparse tundra. Her long, curly brunette hair writhed in the wind like an angry pit of vipers. Alan scowled at the approaching figure, knowing instinctively it was likely his old physician friend on a misguided mission of mercy, then disappeared into his cabin and locked the door.

Inside the cabin, Alan ran his hand through the pale strands of blonde hair hanging like a mop on his head, got on his knees and frantically dug through the plastic bin he stored beneath his bed.

Under the bundles of additional winter clothing, he located the prescription bottle of tranquilizers that would put him out in under twenty minutes. It was empty. He threw it across the room with such force, the plastic cracked and the lid flew off.

His head snapped toward the door with a snarl as Brenda rapped on it insistently.

"Alan, it's Doctor Higgins," her muffled voice announced.

"I came here for solitude! Your company is not welcome!"

"I can't stay out here through the night, "she replied. "I'll die from exposure."

"You'll die of something worse if you come in!" Alan shouted as he backed away from the door, a mixture of fear and anger contorting his face. "Why don't you go back to the hangar?"

Alan knew the hangar wasn't heated, so it wasn't really a viable option. The temperatures would drop below freezing at night and the only insulated thing in the building was an underground tank full of fuel for the planes.

"I've got tranquilizers," Brenda shouted through the thick wooden door.

Alan's face calmed a bit. His eyes darted around the room nervously. He glanced at the hallway leading to the other rooms in the small cabin. With a quick mental calculation, he realized none of the doors would hold against his onslaught if he wasn't sedated. Even at the hangar, she might not be safe from him if he succumbed to the beast inside. He'd designed the inside of the cabin to contain him if the need arose. But it had never really been tested. The beast hadn't really been fed in years, so he wasn't sure it would survive the brunt of insane hunger that would manifest. He walked to the door and opened the cover on the small window.

"Open the pane and pass the tranquilizers inside. If I'm awake enough in twenty minutes, I'll let you in," Alan said, not looking through the window into her eyes. He knew he'd behave foolishly if he got lost in her eyes again.

Without a word, Brenda pushed the full pill bottle through the opening. The bottle clattered to the floor and Alan snapped the small door shut quickly. He snatched the bottle off the floor and went to the faucet to draw some water from his insulated tank. He popped a pill into his mouth and drank down two cups of water with it. The tranquilizers always left him feeling dehydrated afterwards. He thought back to the last time he'd used them before he'd left and felt a stern hollowness occupy his mind.

The compound in Tanzania had been large and practically impenetrable, but the vultures who wanted his blood hadn't let that stop them. It was only when they faced his full wrath that their insane hunt came to an end. Flashes of the slaughter at his clawed hands made him catch his breath. He hadn't thought about that day in so long, he was hoping the details would completely disappear, but the visions of severed limbs, fountains of blood and the copper taste of his victims' flesh made his pulse quicken. His fingertips began to pulse and he feared he'd transform before the tranquilizers took effect. He slowed down his breathing concentrated on the strands of grass growing out on the tundra, blowing in the nearly ever present wind, twisting and shuddering under the omnipresent air currents.

He sat on the floor and assumed a Zen position, breathing and concentrating on the calm wind outside. To her credit, Brenda didn't knock or disturb him for the full twenty minutes. When she did, he knew the pill was taking effect as he felt a bit groggy standing up and walking to the door. Even though he knew he was well under control, he still paused at the door, remembering her scent and the soft touch of her skin against his. He almost didn't open the door.

He flipped the locks open and the steel reinforced Australian buloke barrier swung open easily. As it revealed her to his eyes, he cast them downward to avoid her gaze. He didn't need the recriminations, but worse would be the forgiveness. He couldn't let her into his heart again even if he let her into the building.

Brenda stepped through the opening and gently closed the door behind her.

"Alan, you're looking… lonely," she said.

Alan grunted and walked to the bed. He sat down on it and waved to the lone chair sitting in front of the widescreen television.

"Thank you for the refills, although I rarely need them way out here," Alan said as he slid back across the bed and rested against the wall. His eyelids felt droopy and his limbs heavy, but even thus sedated, he was a danger to others—just not likely to her, at least for the moment.

"I've brought some stronger things along, the strongest ones you've heard of and some new, even heavier experimental sedation if needed," Brenda said.

"Why are you here?" he asked simply. He didn't care how she'd found him. He'd used a good deal of subterfuge to hide his trail, but even he needed supplies every once in a while. He guessed Melanie, his executive assistant, had told her how to find him, so there must be good reason for it besides a desire to reconnect. He was less concerned about the military, industrialists or rogue governments trying to get to him. Those he could handle with the swipe of a claw and a considerable gnashing of teeth.

"I believe we've found a cure," Brenda said. Alan risked a glance up at her face and saw that she was serious. He shuddered as he met her deep blue eyes and quickly looked away. He chuckled.

"We've been through this before," Alan said. "The virus is deeply imbedded in the tissues. I would literally need to die before this virus leaves my body. Even then, it might not."

Brenda nodded and sighed.

"We had to adjust our approach," Brenda said.

"You think you can sneak up on it?" Alan said mockingly. "It's in my brain, the deepest parts of my adrenal medulla. It knows when it's being attacked and defends itself by transforming the host. I assume you remember how this works."

His tone belied the years of research and her doctorates in multiple disciplines. Of course she knew how his sickness worked. It had been her life study, the reason for their meeting in the first place and the reason they'd gotten so close. Too close.

"We think we can apply a patch to allow you to control it, real time, with no ill effects," Brenda said.

"Control it?" Alan laughed bitterly. "Seven hundred and fifty-three, Brenda. Does that number sound familiar?"

"Alan," Brenda replied quietly.

"Trained mercenaries, all at once, sent to subdue me so they could harvest this virus from my organs for their own ignorant and evil uses. Dead in less than an hour according to some estimates. The only ones who escaped never landed on the ground and were over two hundred feet up. I slaughtered everything else. You can't control chaos."

Alan closed his eyes and took a deep breath.

"A reprogrammable drug pump we can resupply through an access port is a permanent solution if it works," Brenda said.

"You're wasting your time," Alan said.

Brenda stood up.

"I was afraid but not surprised you'd say that," she said as she walked toward him.

He frowned and attempted to move, but the drugs were taking effect. He saw her raise her arm and a small dart gun puffed a bit of smoke as the first projectile hit him in the chest. He could feel himself going under and saw her reload the gun, a second dart hitting him in the leg seconds later. Even as he went under, he felt the beast trying to rise from the depths of his psyche. Two more pinches in his limbs and everything went dark.

When the darkness cleared, Alan's head was pounding with the worst headache he'd ever experienced. He rolled onto his side on a cold floor and retched. When the dry heaving finally subsided, his headache had faded to a dull thrum. He took a deep breath and examined his surroundings beyond the splashes of vomit and gray concrete he'd seen so far.

He blinked his eyes as he took in a cavernous, enclosed square hundreds of feet across and just as tall. Far up on one side, there was a glimmer of glass which he assumed was an observation window. The ceiling sported several skylights; they were far enough up that he wasn't sure even he could reach them when the beast took him over. He searched for an opening but only managed a faint outline in one wall he assumed was a reinforced vault-like door likely stronger than the walls themselves which were probably made of reinforced concrete several meters thick. But apart from what looked like an inescapable prison for him, the most intriguing part of the room was Brenda Higgins sitting in an easy chair on the far side of the room reading a book. She looked up from the book and then set it down.

"There are bottles of water behind you to rehydrate," she said.

Alan grunted and grabbed one of the bottles. He opened it and drank the lukewarm water in just a few seconds. A second one disappeared just as quickly. He raised his hand to his forehead and noticed it had no strands of hair hanging down. Feeling around his skull, he noticed faint stubble and a scar on the back of his skull with a small metallic circle imbedded there.

"What have you done to me?" he growled.

"What you wouldn't allow," Brenda said simply.

"You had no right," Alan grumbled. He pulled off the hospital tunic he wore; it was stained with vomit.

"I had no choice," Brenda said.

"You could have left me alone," Alan sneered. He stood up and tested his balance. Squeezing his eyes shut, he re-centered himself and took a deep breath. He walked toward Brenda.

"Seven hundred and fifty-one," Brenda replied as she watched him approach her. She didn't seem concerned even though Alan could go off the deep end and rip her to shreds. Seeing him shirtless brought back a longing for the relationship they'd shared so long ago, reminding her it was out of reach, possibly forever.

They both knew he wouldn't hurt her voluntarily, but alone in an enclosed space with no tranquilizers in sight, Alan felt it was a dangerous chance to take. He wanted to know why she'd taken it.

"Seven hundred and fifty-three," he replied testily.

"No," Brenda replied. "You only severely wounded two of them. They were buried and unconscious beneath their compatriots when the Chinese military recovered them."

"Shit," Alan replied.

"They got what they were after," Brenda said evenly. "But they had no way to control it once they had it. The two infected mercenaries slaughtered all the personnel at the secret base and got out, eliminating three small towns in rural China before they were subdued. Recognizing they were well beyond their understanding, they contacted the only expert on the subject."

"You helped them weaponize it?" Alan was dumbfounded. He'd nearly reached where she was sitting.

"It's difficult to weaponize that kind of chaos. They called me in to cure it. The two mercenaries were sloppy in beast mode. They failed to kill several people and the Chinese found they had an epidemic they didn't understand and couldn't control," Brenda huffed. "They wanted to keep it secret, of course, but I-"

Brenda's words faltered a bit as the emotions took over. She squeezed her eyes shut.

Alan's heart hurt to see her in pain. He felt a bit of anger and the beast knocked on his medulla, but he was surprisingly able to push it back down with ease.

"I thought surely the international community would be able to step in and humanely resolve the crisis. I released the information about what was happening to the world governments. When the Chinese found out..."As Brenda looked into Alan's eyes, tears brimmed her own. "They just slaughtered the infected and called it a hoax."

"I'm sorry," Alan said.

"Three camps, 75,000 or so people. They set off small nuclear devices and called it weapons testing," her voice trailed off and she stared into her memories for a moment, the horror of the consequences of her actions playing over again and again in her mind.

"You can't control the actions of a government like that, Brenda. You did everything you could."

"I let the world know your secret, Alan," Brenda said. "Once it was out of the bag, it was only a matter of time. You're international public enemy number one now."

Alan looked around the room with a new sense of dread. The walls were evidently the least of his worries. Brenda stood up and grasped his arms.

"Alan, if the cure works, they won't kill you," Brenda said, hope shining in her words and her eyes.

"You said you couldn't cure it," Alan said flatly. His face showed despair and defeat instead of anger.

"If you can control it, it can't be unleashed again unless it's intentional. That's as good as curing it."

"You should leave, if I can't control it, you'll be killed," Alan said.

"I don't want to live without you, Alan," Brenda said. Her eyes searched his. "I've felt the same way for twelve years. That's not going to change."

Alan placed his hand on her cheek and smiled for what seemed the first time in years. Time seemed to melt away in that instant; he remembered every glance, every touch and every smile they'd shared.

"Then let's get started. What do I do?"

"Well, for starters, go to that far corner. They're going to try to get the beast to come out and I don't want to be collateral damage to their attempts," Brenda squeezed his arm. "Do whatever you can to keep it bottled up. I've given you every tool I know how to. The rest is up to you."

She stood up on her tiptoes and kissed him. He grabbed her around the waist and held her tight for a longer kiss than she was expecting, but she didn't pull away. Reluctantly, he broke the connection and she rested flat on her feet again.

"Stay safe," he said as he turned and walked to the corner. Brenda let him walk away from her grasp and took a deep breath. She sat back down in the chair and swiveled it to watch. A clear, thick glass wall rose around Brenda along with a thick steel ceiling sliding out from the concrete wall.

"Brenda?" Alan shouted with concern.

"It's OK, Alan. It's for my safety," Brenda sat still, unconcerned.

"All right," Alan said looking up to where the control booth window shielded the other observers from his possible wrath. "Let's get this over with!"

"Commencing," a voice announced over a hidden speaker.

Alan looked around and didn't notice anything. Brenda was looking around as well and didn't see any obvious tests. She stood up and her feet splashed in the accumulating water around her feet. She ran forward and pounded on the glass.

"This wasn't what we agreed to!" She shouted.

"What's wrong?" Alan shouted. Then he noticed the water rising at her feet at an increasing rate.

He ran forward to the glass and hit it with all his might. The thick barrier resisted his attempts.

"You bastards! I'm not going to play your game!" Alan screamed and willed the beast to come forward. That's when he felt a shift in his head as it was flooded with the chemicals from the implant. He raged as a normal man, pounding at the glass as the water rose. Brenda treaded water and grasped at the top edge of the transparent wall, water seeping out from the edge and trickling down the outside. The despair in Alan took over everything as he watched the light go out in Brenda's eyes, her lungs filled with fluid. He fell to his knees, his hands sliding down the slick surface. When he needed the beast, it wouldn't come. Why?

"Now that we know you can be controlled, we can begin your training," a man's voice announced over the speakers. Three uniformed men walked into the room, the two in the lead armed with tranquilizer guns. The officer behind them smiled as he entered.

With reckless intent, Alan leapt to his feet and rushed them. The two men fired and the tranquilizer darts hit their mark. Alan fell to his knees again and continued crawling until his body stopped responding to his mental commands.

"She was innocent! You didn't have to kill her…" he gasped.

"Well, Mister Jeffries, someone had to pay the price for your crimes. Why not lose something you cared about when so many others have lost what they cared for?" The officer smiled as Alan continued to struggle against the tranquilizers. "Your resistance is impressive, even when you're not in combat mode."

"I'll never fight for you," Alan mumbled.

"Pain is an amazing incentivizer for troops and others. That device in your head can reward and punish just as easily as it can control your combat effectiveness. It had additional functions your hapless doctor friend was unaware of," the officer said as he glanced up casually at the floating form in the water. "She truly was innocent to the last."

Alan reached for the officer with a surprising swiftness that caught the others off guard. He nearly reached him before taking two more darts and they jumped on him, finally bringing him down. He fell into the depths of darkness a second time.

Again unsure of how much time had passed, Alan woke up in his bed in his mansion in New York. He felt his head and there was a bare growth of stubble there along with the bump of the port in his skull. He took his time sitting up. A note addressed to him sat on the nightstand next to his bed. He reached for it with slightly trembling fingers and flipped it open.

"You're under constant surveillance, Mister Jeffries. Any missteps and we'll activate the pain protocol of your implant, turning it off only at our leisure. You'll receive orders soon. Keep your strength up. You'll need it."

Alan dropped the note on the floor, got up and walked to the front room of his mansion. He looked around and could see the changes made, the small surveillance cameras added to his domicile. His senses picked them up and noted each location. He calmly made himself some breakfast and consumed it rapidly, fighting back the nausea he felt having consumed solid food for the first time in what he felt may be days or possibly weeks.

He finished his meal, put the dishes in the dishwasher and walked back into the bedroom. He bent down to pick up the note, set it back on the nightstand and grabbed the lamp, quickly pulling the cord from the back of it. He shoved the live wire into the port in the back of his skull. He held it there until the pain made him pass out.

Knowing his healing abilities hadn't been affected by the implant, he knew he'd only be out a matter of seconds, maybe as long as a minute or two. Not long enough for them to mount a physical offensive.

He awoke to the smell of burnt flesh and a dull, throbbing ache deep inside his skull. He got up and winced, noting the pain was already lessening and would be completely gone within minutes. He looked directly into one of the cameras in his room.

"Your first mistake was assuming you could control chaos," Alan growled into the camera. "Your second mistake was killing the only reason I controlled my darkest impulses. You want to see the beast? I'll make sure he spreads to every corner of the world."

With a roar, Alan's body transformed. His arms lengthened, sharp claws protruding from his fingertips. He grew another six inches in height as his legs increased in girth two-fold. His feet became clawed paws. Hair pushed up through every pore. His head lengthened, his mouth protruding into a wolfish snout. He looked at the camera one last time with large yellow eyes and grinned, saliva dripping from his canine teeth. Throwing his head back, Alan howled, then leaped out of his bedroom window to the grounds one floor below and disappeared into the woods surrounding his estate.

PROGRESSION

iana walked out into the hallway and was shocked to see her old elementary reading teacher sitting there in a wheelchair. She brushed her blonde hair back behind one ear and smiled.

"Missus Cooney, what a pleasant surprise," she said and held out her hand.

The older woman grabbed her hand enthusiastically and beamed. Her gray curls looked exactly as Diana remembered them all those years ago. Her green eyes twinkled.

"Diana, I just knew you'd turn out to be someone who helped people," the woman gushed. "Please, call me Christine."

Diana nodded awkwardly and took her hand back.

"So, Christine, what brings you to Airdale?"

"Well, I'm here primarily for you, dear."

Diana frowned. She looked around to see if there was a camera and some kind of reality trick going on. There didn't seem to be. She sat down on a bench in the hallway.

"Christine, we're a hospice, an end of life facility. While I can see you're in a wheelchair, it doesn't seem like you're facing an end of life scenario. Has there been some kind of diagnosis for you?"

Christine chuckled and shook her head.

"I told you, I'm here for you," Christine said and waved toward the end of the hall with the stub of a left hand toward the library. "Now, if you could help me, it's become difficult to maneuver in a manual without the hand here."

Diana blinked at the stub. Surely, she'd just had her hands held by Christine. Had she missed her teacher's absent hand somehow? Perhaps it had been from the shock of seeing this part of her past here and now. She shook her head, stood up and walked behind the wheelchair.

"I'd be happy to help, Christine," Diana said and pushed the elder lady down the hall. "So, who's your doctor?"

They continued down the hall, Diana looking out the windows at the spring flowers blooming in the sun.

"Oh," Christine said. "Doctor Hammond was wonderful, always took the extra time to see how I was feeling, not just roll me through the office like I was on an assembly line. He had the most wonderful smile and his nurse, Brenda, was the nicest young lady you could ever chat with. They were very personable."

"Would that be Doctor Hammond from Brightsville?" Diana asked.

"That's him. Such a wonderful man," Christine said and sighed.

Diana stopped the wheelchair and looked behind her. Normally there was a little more traffic in the hallway, but that wasn't the only peculiar thing about the day. Doctor Hammond was a psychiatrist at Brightsville Sanitarium. He didn't normally refer patients under his care here to Airdale. But then, he'd stopped his practice years ago. He was one of the first doctors Diana had interacted with when she started working at Airdale.

"Christine," Diana said gently. "I think Doctor Hammond retired several years ago."

"Yes," Christine nodded. "I haven't seen him in a long time."

"Oh," Diana breathed a sigh of relief. Christine was clearly just reminiscing. Diana began to push the wheelchair again and the doors to the library opened automatically. They rolled past the front desk and Diana noticed there was no one manning the station. She glanced around the small library and realized it was completely empty of people.

"Well, Christine, who's your doctor now?" Diana said as she left Christine's wheel chair and walked behind the front desk looking for the librarian.

"Oh, dear, I don't need one anymore since I passed away," Christine said. Diana had just poked her head around the corner of the small hallway when she stopped and turned to look back at Christine. Her teacher was no longer there. Diana rushed back to where she'd left the wheelchair and it was gone. She darted around the rows of the library, but Christine was nowhere to be found.

"What the hell," Diana whispered. She walked back out the door to the library and the hallway was empty. Maybe someone with two functioning hands and arms could maneuver a manual wheelchair away that fast, but Christine didn't and couldn't. Diana walked back past the other office doors, stopping at each one and finding no one there. Neither Christine nor the regular employees of the hospice were anywhere to be found. Christine shuddered and walked back to her office.

As she walked through her office door, she snapped her fingers. She'd been leaving earlier to get something. She paused at the door and tried to think of what it was she meant to retrieve. The only thing that came to mind was her car keys. She walked back out the door and found Mrs. Cooney waiting there for her, sitting in her wheelchair.

"Oh!" Diana exclaimed. This time she noticed the old woman was also missing her left foot. A stump hung off the edge of the wheelchair. Diana processed this for a moment and realized she just hadn't noticed it before. Now it made perfect sense why Christine was in a wheelchair.

"Hello again, Diana!" Christine gushed and held out her right hand. After a pause, Diana grasped her right hand with both of hers and smiled.

"Missus Cooney," Diana replied.

"Remember, I told you to call me Christine," she chided and Diana blushed.

"Of course you did," Diana replied. She looked up and down the hall again, but it remained as vacant as before. She stepped behind the wheelchair and pushed her teacher toward the library.

"Such a beautiful summer day," Christine commented.

"It's still spring, Christine," Diana replied and looked out the windows as they walked. The grass had turned brown and most of the flowers had wilted in the oppressive summer heat. Diana stopped pushing the wheelchair and walked to the window. She pressed her hand to the glass and felt the heat from the summer sun radiating through it.

"Time marches on," Christine said. "No rest for the weary... most of the time."

Diana stared out the window, looking up and down the normally active sidewalk a few hundred yards away. The street beyond was similarly vacant.

"Seems like everyone's resting today," Diana replied. She turned back to Mrs. Cooney and the old woman had disappeared again. "Oh, for goodness sake."

Diana walked back to her office and shut the door behind her. She sat down at her desk and moved things on her desk looking for her car keys. They weren't in the drawers either. She stood up and looked on the bookshelf next to the chair she had for patients and clients. Her purse sat on top. She sighed in relief and grabbed it. She opened the purse and found medical gauze stained with blood. She dropped the purse on the guest chair. The gauze fell onto the floor and rolled out across the room, leaving a blood stained tail behind it.

There was a knock on the door and Diana jumped. She glanced at the gauze on the floor and shook her head.

"What a shitty practical joke," she murmured as she walked to the door. She opened it to find Christine there again. Both of the old woman's legs were gone, further up the leg this time. She sported two stumps that barely reached the edge of the seat. Her left arm was now missing all the way up past the elbow.

"Diana, can you push me down to the library?" Christine asked, smiling. She said it with a slight slur and Diana noticed her old teacher had a few teeth missing. Without a word, Diana walked behind the chair and pushed it down the hall. There was a slight chill in the air. With each step, goose bumps multiplied on Diana's arms and it wasn't just from the cooler air in the hallway. She glanced out the window and saw the trees nearly barren, leaves piled up on the grass.

"It's not every day I get a dead teacher from my past visiting me at my office," Diana said.

"The mind works in mysterious ways, doesn't it Diana?" Christine replied, her speech punctuated by hisses between her missing teeth. Diana didn't respond but continued pushing her teacher down the hall. They went through the automatic doors again. As before, there was no one to greet them in the library.

"Could you push me over to the fiction section?" Christine asked. "I always loved the creation of stories from nothing but the mind's eye."

Diana pushed the wheelchair to the section three rows deep and stopped. Christine turned around and looked up at her.

"You can let go now. I wanted to know if you'd look up Alice in Wonderland for me. It's one of the classics," Christine asked.

"If I let go of the chair, you'll disappear again," Diana said. "I'm afraid to let you go."

"Get me the book," Christine said. "I won't go away until it's time for me to go."

Diana stood unmoving for a few seconds or even a few minutes, she wasn't sure how time passed anymore. Finally, she released the wheelchair and stepped toward the bookshelf. Looking along the shelf, she recognized every book there. She'd read them all. There was nothing there she hadn't opened and devoured when she was younger. Her reading had fallen off lately, but every once in a while she picked up a newer book. They were all here. She moved along the row and found Lewis Carroll's Alice in Wonderland. She pulled the book from the shelf and turned toward Christine, who remained there in the wheelchair, unchanged from before.

"You're still here," Diana said.

"Of course, I am," Christine responded and smiled her broken smile. "You're almost ready."

Christine reached for the book with her right hand. Diana handed it to her. Christine sat back comfortably in the wheelchair and opened the book with her good hand, steadying it with the stump of her left arm.

"Almost ready for what?"

"You see me reading?" Christine asked.

Diana nodded and frowned. "Do you need some alone time?"

"No," Christine chuckled. "I can read, I can write, operate an electric wheelchair, a computer, a vehicle if I like with the right modifications. I can do most anything with some obvious exceptions, but even prosthetics and technology can accommodate most anything life can throw at you."

Diana nodded her head. "I work in the medical field. I keep up on all the latest breakthroughs, even though in my particular work, I only see people when they're beyond the help of most advances."

"Is it fair to say, you think I could do most anything I wanted to with the help of technology and some devices?"

"Surely, there's retraining and physical therapy that can help you adapt to most any challenges you might come across," Diana cocked her head to the side. "Am I being fired? Or maybe I'm getting transferred to a physical therapy unit? Is that it?"

Christine smiled. "Not exactly, but that could be part of it, if you choose."

"If I choose?"

"If you're ready," Christine leaned forward, holding the book on her lap. "Diana, do you think you're ready?"

"Maybe," Diana said. Christine peered into her eyes and Diana felt as if her old mentor was measuring her soul for worthiness. Christine shrugged.

"Well, it's your decision, I'm just here at your whim," Christine muttered. She handed the book to Diana. "Well after the Rabbit Hole and just beyond the Pool of Tears, as would seem most appropriate."

Diana took the book from Christine and opened it to the first chapter, Down the Rabbit Hole. She hesitated and looked up. Christine had disappeared. Diana closed the book and looked around briefly. She shrugged her shoulders and decided it didn't matter if her old teacher was here any longer. Perhaps her work was done.

Diana walked to one of the tables and set the book down

again. She read through the first chapter, reminiscing about one of her favorite books. She didn't understand the significance of it compared to what she was going through, although she had to admit it was strange. She plowed quickly through the next chapter and when she got to the first page of chapter three, the center of the book had been hollowed out and inside it were her car keys. She lifted them carefully from the center of the book. They dripped with blood.

Suddenly, she was no longer sitting in the library, but held the keys out in front of her while she sat in her car. Her first instinct was to put the keys in the ignition, but she hesitated. In slow motion, her hand moved toward the ignition. Time seemed to standstill and her breath stopped. All sound ceased and her hand trembled as it moved inches toward placing the key into the receptacle.

Tears fell from her cheeks and she jerked her hand backward. She opened the car door, ran toward the building and went inside. Through the empty corridors she ran, crying all the way though she wasn't sure why.

Diana burst through her office door and shut it quickly behind her. She collapsed into her chair and put her head down on her desk, sobbing uncontrollably.

"Perhaps you weren't ready," Christine's voice whispered. Diana raised her head and saw her teacher sitting in the guest chair next to her desk. She was absently rolling the bloody gauze up with her two perfectly normal hands and then placed the gauze back in Diana's purse.

"I'm scared," Diana said. She wiped the tears from her face and looked away from the first teacher who really cared about her.

"I know," Christine said. "And that's perfectly normal, but..."

As Christine's voice faded, Diana looked up and saw Christine pointing at the calendar on the wall. The pages started falling from it, month after month drifting slowly to the floor.

"Time marches on, Diana," Christine whispered. "You can join the mad tea party for a while or you can miss the story altogether and reach The End far faster. Winter is upon us. There isn't much time."

Christine got up and placed Diana's purse back up on the bookshelf and walked out of the room. Diana watched her go and saw snowflakes falling outside the windows in the hallway before Christine shut the door quietly behind her.

Diana watched Christine's silhouette beyond the frosted glass of her office door fade from sight. She looked back at her desk and sniffled.

"I'm not ready," Diana said and looked through her desk. She found her appointment book and pulled it out. She went through her appointment book and found April. All the appointments she remembered holding were in there, but when she searched through the pages after April, there were no appointments. The empty pages turned to dust in her hands.

Diana stood up from her desk and a crackling sound drew her attention to the clock high up on the wall. It was smoking and the second hand was slowing as it struggled around the face of the clock.

"I'm not ready!" She screamed at the clock. It continued to smoke and flames erupted from the face of the clock.

Diana looked down at the bloody keys and grabbed them. She opened the door and saw Christine sitting in the wheelchair, left arm and two legs missing again. Christine looked up at her sadly.

"There's not much time left at all," Christine said, then she closed her eyes and rapidly decayed, becoming a skeleton and then nothing but dust in a matter of seconds. The paint on the walls began to fray with age and neglect. Diana ran back through the doors that led through her building. They hung halfway off the hinges. As she ran through the building toward the parking lot, the whole building seemed to fall apart around her.

Her car gleamed like new in the parking lot. She climbed into the car and shut the door. She looked at the Airdale Hospice Center and it seemed to fall to dust before her eyes. The trees and grass faded from full color to gray. She looked at the keys and then the ignition switch.

"Perhaps it's for the best..." she heard her husband's voice whisper into her ear. She grimaced and stuck the key into the ignition. She cried out in pain as she awoke in the hospital bed.

"Diana!" Mike shouted in relief, tears in his eyes.

She tried to speak, but the tube in her throat prevented it. She grasped her husband's hand with her right hand, realizing quickly that it was the only limb she had left. A doctor put his stethoscope to her chest and then flashed a light into her eyes.

"She's back," he said, the shock apparent in the doctor's voice. "Somehow, she's back."

"What a long sleep you've had," her husband said. She looked into his brown eyes and saw true relief and love there.

"Oh, I've had such a curious dream," she thought as he caressed her cheek.

BALANCE

Helena walked into the room, a slim, six-inch knife tucked into the back waistband of her panties beneath the navy blue pencil skirt. She wore a matching navy blue coat with a dazzling white blouse underneath. She looked pristine and professional as always. No one outside this office would ever suspect her heart was darker than her suit.

Her partner in crime, Alan, sat oblivious at his desk working at his laptop computer. Helena admired his strong jaw line and appreciated the receding hairline as she felt it showed his maturity. His tan suit coat hung on a coat tree to his right. His perfectly starched, wrinkle free white shirt matched his outward personality— the one he showed legal peers and clients. The dark green patterned tie was unremarkable except that it went well with the tan suit. Helena cleared her throat and Alan looked up.

"Helena!" Alan stood up suddenly, not from fear but surprise. "You look fantastic! Uh, did we have an appointment?"

Helena smirked at the slight twitch in his crotch. She'd surprised Alan before with an afternoon tryst and clearly he was anticipating another such event.

"Alan, I'm sorry for just dropping in, but I've been troubled," Helena said as she stood by the seat across from Alan. She smiled pleasantly and Alan frowned slightly, his disappointment in the apparent platonic visit apparent. He sighed and quickly recovered; flashing the dazzling smile that always set their victims at ease.

"How can I help?" Alan sat back in his chair and folded his hands in his lap, perhaps to rearrange what had been growing there.

"We've done some wicked acts together, Alan."

Alan blinked and then raised his eyebrows.

"Oh, yes we have. Here I was thinking this wasn't going to be a conjugal visit." Alan chuckled and loosened his tie.

Helena loosened the button on her coat and walked forward. Alan leered openly. Then Helena sat down in the chair directly opposite him. Alan cocked his head curiously.

"I'm afraid I refer to our off premises activities," Helena said and sighed. A brief frown touched Alan's face before he controlled all his expressions. He closed the lid on his laptop.

"I don't know what you mean," he said impassively. His eyes darted to her neck and chest, no longer appraising but searching.

"I'm not wearing a wire, Alan. I haven't gone to the police and don't intend to. We've killed together and I don't think I can bargain my way out of that, especially Lake Tahoe. I mean, you didn't do anything but watch me kill that couple. The luring of them to the room, drugging them and tying them up was all my doing. I remember the distinct thrill seeing the fear on their faces when they awoke, seeing you just across the room, sitting and watching, while I stood before them totally naked wielding a machete and wire clippers. Completely dismembering their bodies while they were still alive until, of course, they weren't. The tourniquets prolonged that process for a delicious two hours, though. But that was all my planning and execution, if you'll forgive the phrase. That was totally on me."

Alan blinked but his face remained impassive.

"Why are you here?" Alan moved his chair forward to the desk. There was a barely audible click as the door to his office locked. Helena smiled. She'd already advised the secretary to leave for the day, a practice they'd set in motion a dozen or more times before, giving them ultimate privacy for carnal activities. Helena enjoyed Alan's touch, his animal nature while in the throes of passion. There was asphyxiation, bruising and sometimes blood. She was going to miss that.

"There's a struggle within me, Alan. Good versus evil. I need your input on what I should do."

Alan pursed his lips and then stood up. He walked over to an oak filing cabinet and opened the bottom drawer. He retrieved a bottle of Belvenie and two glasses.

"The struggle between good and evil is a classic one. It's a rousing philosophical debate even in our modern times. The give and take, the yin and yang. There are so many examples in literature you could reference. Why come to me?"

Alan sat back down and poured two glasses. He set one in front of Helena and took the other. He sat down and savored the aroma of the fine scotch and sipped a small amount into his mouth.

"Have you ever struggled with balance?" Helena asked. She took the glass and enjoyed a small sip.

"I don't struggle," he said simply, sitting back in the chair. "I never doubt my actions. I'm confident in my path."

"Even Toronto?" Helena sipped her drink again and smiled.

"Of course, I don't know what you mean by Toronto, but regardless, when you are certain about who you are there's never a question. Have you come to doubt who you are?"

"The children in Toronto," Helena said setting her glass on the desk and putting her hands in her lap. "What happened to them caused a glimmer of doubt in my core. Innocence taken so early. I'm having trouble resolving it in my mind."

Alan sniffed his drink again. He twirled it around, carefully considering his response. Helena smiled again. She knew he still suspected she was wired up. This game was fun.

"There's good in this world and there's evil. Each has its place," Alan said as he stood up and walked around the desk to her. "Stand up and remove your coat, please."

Helena complied and gave him a smoldering smile. She dropped her coat onto the chair. As she did so, her eyes caught note of the easily removable carpet, something she'd helped Alan with only a few months before when they'd dispatched a particularly nosy reporter. She knew where all the cleaning supplies were, the spare carpet and duplicate furniture if needed. There was a particularly deep ravine outside of town that had several dumped bodies at the bottom of it, a fact she could thank Alan for alerting her to. If anyone besides Alan could get away with a crime right here in his own office, it was Helena.

"Think of the elegant balance of the two," Alan continued as he walked around her, caressing her back through the blouse, checking for the tell tale sign of a wire. "Remove your skirt too."

"You are insatiable, Alan," Helena said and lowered the zipper and stepped daintily out of the tight skirt, setting it next to the coat. Alan lingered for a bit, taking a deep breath as he perused her beautifully tanned and toned legs. They had been wrapped around him dozens of times in this office, at his home and in hotel rooms across the world.

"Neither good nor evil are wrong. They need each other to exist," Alan said as he walked back to his chair and sat down.

"Remove your blouse."

Helena undid the buttons to the blouse and stripped the garment back off her shoulders slowly, revealing a low cut, navy blue lace bra. Alan nodded admiringly.

"If there was no evil, would there be good? I propose they would both perish together leaving the world limp and formless," Alan said, again adjusting himself in his pants obviously enjoying Helena's sleek form. "A colorful world suddenly devoid of passion and promise would seem dull. A grey, lifeless dimension would permeate the planet. Surely, you wouldn't want that?"

"Of course not, Alan." Helena winked and removed her bra. A flush of adrenaline flowed through her as Alan nodded approvingly at her nearly bare form. She picked the glass up, took another sip and then set it back on the desk. "I want a world full of color, passion and promise. I didn't mean to make you worry."

Helena walked slowly around the desk, her hips swaying suggestively in the filtered sunlight streaming in through the frosted office windows. She bent down and kissed Alan lightly on the lips as he gently grazed her exposed breast. She walked behind him and massaged his shoulders. He relaxed into her touch.

"A world in perfect balance leads to some of the most delicious developments," Alan murmured. Helena chuckled.

"We've done so many interesting things together, Alan. Things to make the pulse race in various flavors, exciting so many different senses." Helena dug deep with her fingers, making Alan groan. "You remember our first time, abroad in Attenborough. The way you talked me through holding that man's head down while you carved out his tongue?"

"How could I forget?" Alan said softly.

"The sensation of the warm blood flowing forth from his mouth, spraying us both as he struggled in the restraints is my first precious memory of that time," Helena said, feeling the excitement of the moment making her heart beat faster. She had so much to thank Alan for, the freedom to explore her darker side and the independence of knowing how to get away with it so she could do it again and again.

"I can still hear his struggling gasps and garbled screams as you plunged the knife into his body dozens of times, prolonging his suffering for hours. Had we remembered smelling salts, I truly think we could have gotten another half hour out of him. These are special times, Alan. Getting to reminisce about the joys we've explored together."

She cocked her head for a moment as she kneaded the flesh of Alan's shoulders in her hands. She would miss these times. Hunting together was always fun, but there was always the possibility of betrayal hiding behind every action, every experience. Their last time together in Toronto had been a bit of touch and go. She'd hesitated, perhaps one too many times. Alan had voiced his disappointment and it seemed no apology from her at the time could assuage his concern. If she was him, she would've been planning her own demise by now. There was too much chance for a conscience to get the better of your partner, too much chance for a slip of the tongue revealing details to an impartial party. Quite simply, there were too many loose ends. She sighed as she resigned herself to go through with it. She would have to figure out how to deal with her own loss another time.

"I've missed our little departures," Alan replied. "It's been nearly three weeks since our last adventure. Even longer since you last pleasured me in my office."

Helena observed the bulge in his pants grow ever so slightly more. A pang of regret clouded her face. The intensity of their sexual liaisons had always been particularly exhilarating. An afternoon or evening filled with the bondage, the pain, the pleasure and wondering constantly if you'd actually live through the experience. Dancing on the edge of death was an experience she'd truly miss. She made a mental note to find some underground establishment that could cater to that particular diversion.

"If it was too often, it would become commonplace, Alan. Then it wouldn't be as special anymore, would it?"

"Depravity needs its outlet, my sweet. Even as the pursuit and flow of riches pulses through my mind, so too does the need to expand my sexual prowess. As I'm sure you've now learned all too well, the body has needs. We crave experiences that enrich our senses. Those of us at the top of the food chain require the sustenance of pleasure and pain."

"Is that what you consider us, Alan? The top of the food chain?"

Alan loosened his belt and undid the clasp holding his pants together.

"I know we are," Alan said. "Prey needs predators to thin the herd, keep their numbers down and eliminate the weak. If you understand anything about the world, our place in it is key."

Helena removed Alan's tie and let it drop to the floor, returning her fingers to massage the sides of his neck.

"Just like the muscles of the body need balance, tensing and relaxing, breaking and building, I understand the world perfectly," Helena said. With lightning speed she dropped her right hand behind her back, pulled out the sharp knife and whipped it around to Alan's neck.

"Helena?" Alan whispered. The muscle in his right arm twitched almost unnoticeably, but Helena caught it, pressing the blade a little closer to the skin, bringing forth a single drop of blood. Alan knew the speed with which she could dispatch him. She'd been needled by him more than a dozen times to strike without hesitation, without fear.

"Toronto, Alan," Helena said. "We put too much evil on the ledger. I've decided good needs to win today."

"There's so much good in the world already!" Alan shouted. Helena turned the tip of the blade, carving a small divot in the tender skin of his neck, but not deep enough to be fatal. Alan gripped the armrests of the chair, steadying himself for what Helena knew would be a last ditch effort when he felt he had no other choice.

"Is there Alan?" Helena asked warmly. "We've both delighted in the dark politics abounding in the world. Money rules and goodness drools, wasn't that your clever saying? I remember laughing heartily with you then."

"You've killed at my side!" Alan said. "You're just as evil as I am!"

"Tomorrow perhaps, darling," Helena said and shoved the blade through his throat, bisecting the larynx and severing the carotid artery. "But today, I must strike for good."

Helena held Alan's head as he gasped for breath, his hand clutching at his neck, blood spewing forth and drenching the front of his trembling body. The crimson liquid spilled forth, staining the pristine white fabric of his shirt. Helena reveled in the stark contrast between the two colors, so beautiful in its own right. Brushing his hand away for a moment, she wrapped her right arm around his neck and dropped the dagger to the floor. She closed her eyes and delighted in the sensation of the warm fluid spurting from his throat onto her forearm even as his hands gripped her arm trying to dislodge it. He pushed against the desk, trying to get leverage to push her off of him, but she held firm until his trembling subsided and she could feel his fingers on her arm weaken. There would be bruising there on her skin, but given the cleanup she had planned, no one would miss him for days. The bruising, if she was ever even questioned, would be gone. For now, she could enjoy the bittersweet last moments of his life as it slipped away in the grip of her arms.

She considered for a moment that maybe she'd been too compassionate. Didn't he deserve a long death to pay for the evil he'd done? The odds of him escaping were too great. She knew his prowess as a combatant would've been too much even for her if she didn't have the element of surprise. He jerked one last time as his body gave up the fight. She knew his mind would be around for a few precious seconds after he could no longer move.

"Shh," Helena whispered. "It's all for balance."

What Remains

King Dolnar walked into the charred and destroyed remains of the throne room for what seemed the hundredth time. He carefully navigated the broken stones and broken beams to the front of the cavernous room. Big enough to fit a dragon, his father had said when he built it decades earlier. Unfortunately, he'd been only too accurate.

His feet came to rest at the foot of the shattered throne. The scent of the room still made him gag, but the smell had faded. Even so, his memory of that day came flooding back to his mind.

Queen Alorra had been sitting here in his stead while he chased the winged beast of the neighboring mountains. He'd failed to anticipate the giant lizard's intelligence, thinking it no more than an oversized winged rat. But it knew all along where he resided and, somehow, what he cared for most. Oddly enough, the Queen's death was the price he paid for success.

"And yet, I feel I've lost everything," he whispered to the empty room, appealing to the ghosts of the great hall.

Ten months had passed since the attack from the great wyrm, Charos; an attack in direct response to Dolnar's assault on the beast's lair in the mountains, the crushing of the dragon's eggs and slaughter of her fledgling young. They'd struck while she was out hunting and feeding, assaulting the King's lands yet again. Dozens of assaults from above had seen the disappearance of hundreds of livestock, the burning of farms and loss of many villagers. They were the simple yet brutal actions of a mother caring for her growing brood.

He'd done what he needed to do for his kingdom. Destroy the nest and, ultimately, the dragon. He'd expected to do the last act there on the mountains, not chasing the rising smoke from his own castle through the night. While the beast eventually died from the wounds she took attacking the keep, she had already exacted her revenge by then.

Why hadn't his love sought refuge in the dungeons below or in the escape tunnels? Why she had remained here in the great hall he'd never know. Everyone here had perished long before his rescue party arrived.

As always, he hadn't been gone more than fifteen minutes when Sir Bendell found him. His second hand emerged from the broken hallways beyond, crawling amidst the fallen stones with some difficulty. The leg injury he received during the destruction of the dragon hive had left him with a noticeable limp.

"Sire," Sir Bendell began.

"Save it, Ben," Dolnar replied. "I don't need the lecture."

Sir Bendell pursed his lips and nodded. He looked around at the charred room and then back at Dolnar, his eyebrows raised. Dolnar sighed.

"It's time, Ben."

"Time sire? To rebuild?"

"No, I weary of this burden," Dolnar said. He walked to the edge of the ruins and looked down into the town square where Charos' curiously preserved body lay. "It's time Evan took the reins."

"But sire, he's only sixteen," Sir Bendell scoffed.

"Was I so much older when I ascended the throne?" Dolnar replied, still looking down at the fallen foe.

"But… you were battle tested! A leader!"

"Evan has been in the field for two years. Do you forget it was Evan who saved your life in the hive?" Dolnar turned and glared at Sir Bendell.

"I apologize, sire," Sir Bendell replied looking down. "I'm not ready to see you go, I'm afraid."

"Ben, don't you see? My soul left months ago. My body just hasn't realized it yet," Dolnar turned back to the window. "Perhaps a fresher perspective, a younger mind can solve the riddle of the dead dragon."

"As you wish, sire," Sir Bendell said. "But where will you go? Will you remain to advise the Prince?"

"We, Ben, will be traveling to the North. It is time to enjoy wandering the wastes and finding adventure again. Somewhere far from this kingdom is our destination. We're leaving the past behind."

Sir Bendell walked slowly to the edge of the room, staring out at the town below. The morning sun struggled to pierce the clouds above, leaving the buildings below bathed in a dreary light, the morning mist failing to burn away. He rested his hand on the column still standing there, holding up a non-existent roof.

"The beast has not decayed, sire. What if it isn't truly dead?"

"Then the new king will have a different puzzle to solve. How to kill the unkillable," Dolnar muttered. He turned to his advisor. "Make the announcement. Arrange the coronation. We leave in a fortnight."

"Sire!" Sir Bendell protested. "That's barely enough time to alert the other kingdoms!"

"Then, my good man, you'd better hop to it."

Dolnar turned to Sir Bendell, who had not moved from the spot. He frowned as he noticed Sir Bendell's gaze remained on the scene below. He looked to where his good friend stared and saw the cause for his attention. The upturned crow headdress was unmistakable—Ariastheni had returned with her brood of witches to visit his court again. He watched them examine the dragon's inert body. Ariastheni placed her hand on the flesh of the beast and a bright green glow emanated from the spot. Ariastheni removed her hand and then looked up at Dolnar, unerringly finding him amidst the ruined part of the castle. When she looked at him, he shuddered. It was as if she peered into his very soul. He refused to shy away from her gaze. After what seemed like hours, but could have been no more than a few minutes, Ariastheni dropped her eyes and walked away from the dragon, heading to the right. Dolnar sighed. She meant to have an audience with the king.

"Ariastheni beckons, Ben," he said as he turned away. "Let's go see what the old witch has to say."

"Sire," Sir Bendell responded as he turned and watched King Dolnar retreat from the room with haste. "If you but wish it, I shall send the old hag away."

As they deftly navigated the fallen debris, King Dolnar laughed.

"Send her away?" the King responded as he reached the intact part of the hallway. "Why should I do that when it was I who sent for her?"

"Her sorcery has no place in civilized society," Sir Bendell responded and spat on the ground. "Superstitious nonsense."

"In months of consultation with all the clergy from our kingdom and those surrounding us, not a single person came forth with any credible theories about why the dragon remains," Dolnar said as he strode toward the banquet hall. "I sent for her shortly after normal means failed. Why it took her six months to respond is beyond me, but now that's she's here, I will certainly lend her an ear."

"Sire, you're leaving in a fortnight. Surely you can leave the matter to your son," Sir Bendell murmured.

Dolnar stopped in his tracks and turned on his advisor who shuffled to a stop.

"I'm the King," Dolnar said in a tone dark and dangerous. "Until that changes, keep your head about you lest you lose it permanently."

Sir Bendell paled. "Of course, sire," he said and bowed his head.

King Dolnar nodded at his friend and smiled warmly. "Good." He patted him on the shoulder and turned away, heading for the banquet hall again.

Sir Bendell stood motionless for a few seconds and stared after his king. He blinked a few times, shook his head and then followed after him.

When they reached the banquet hall, the King sat in the slightly raised great chair he currently called his throne and awaited the arrival of his invited guests. Sir Bendell walked in stiffly and sat to the king's right hand at the long banquet table.

A runner came in from the gate and bowed as he entered the room.

"Sire," the young man said. "There are some strange people—"

"Yes, Tommy, a strange woman with a crow on her head and four equally strangely dressed women wish to see me. Send them in."

"But how," Tommy began and then immediately bowed again. "Of course, sire. As you command."

The boy turned straight away and ran full speed toward the front of the castle.

The king turned to Sir Bendell.

"That boy's got a lot of promise," Dolnar said. "Quick thinking, fast on his feet. Does Evan have a squire yet?"

"No, your grace," Sir Bendell responded. "That is, the last one took a bad spill and has become lame. We had to move him to the kitchens."

"Well, he certainly can't take Tommy's place with a bum leg. But see to it that Tommy gets a move to Evan's side. Do Evan some good to see how quick a commoner can be. Keep him on his toes."

Before long, the feathered headdress of Ariastheni bowed low upon entering the room. She was followed by four more women dressed in various skins, furs and feathered attire. People of the wild, they were called in more polite circles. Others called them witches, sorcerers and consorts of the devil. The four women kneeled down and Ariastheni stood in front of them, still bowing her head.

"Arise, Ariastheni," King Dolnar said and she raised her head, her sparkling blue eyes taking his breath away. Faint tendrils of her golden hair peeked out around the headdress. He closed his eyes and took a breath. She was always a temptation but never a prize that could be won without being taken against her will. She'd always been off limits even before the King had met Alorra. Still, she made something stir deep in his soul and in his loins.

"My king, I have come at your request," Ariastheni said. The statement was plain, quiet and sullen. It wasn't the usual bubbly, upbeat song of words she normally set forth when she came to court.

"You're troubled," Dolnar said. "That much is plain. What troubles you?"

"You sent for me and I at first did not come because I thought there was nothing I could do for you. Dragons, after all, are magical and my expertise is in the natural. Still, I know something of curses," Ariastheni stepped forward and leaned on one of the low-backed chairs on her side of the table.

"A curse?" Sir Bendell stood up. "Of all the preposterous-"

"Sit down, Ben. I don't need your counsel just yet," Dolnar said with a chuckle.

Flustered, Sir Bendell bowed to his king and sat down. He frowned at Ariastheni.

"What is the curse?" King Dolnar asked.

"I don't know," Ariastheni said. Sir Bendell strangled a reply but still made a small squeak of contempt at the woman.

"I don't understand." Dolnar frowned.

"I can tell you who is behind the curse, but I know not the nature of it. Only that it involves the beast in the courtyard," Ariastheni replied, bowing her head once more.

"Who, then, is behind the curse?" Dolnar said leaning forward.

"The spirits whispered to me the name Zettelek," Ariastheni said almost unsure of the pronunciation.

"The sorcerer?" Dolnar sat back with a groan.

"We put him to death a decade ago." Sir Bendell spat on the floor in disgust. "He put his dark magic to the ill of this kingdom one too many times and got his just reward. Anyone wielding magic is just as tainted by evil."

"Surely, no one of non-magical persuasion could do any evil then, lest all be accused of being the same sort," Ariastheni retorted.

"Enough, you two," Dolnar growled. "We're not here to debate the nature of all magic, just the nature of the magic surrounding Charos."

Dolnar turned and shouted at an open doorway to the left of him. "Fetch the Royal Scribe!"

"Yes, your majesty!" came the shouted reply from an unseen servant. Running footsteps could be heard disappearing into the distance.

"Why did you come?" Dolnar asked.

"Well," Ariastheni looked around at her companions, confused. "You sent for me."

"Six months ago," Dolnar said. "As you're not a subject of my immediate kingdom, I could not compel you to come forth by penalty of death, so…"

Ariastheni looked down. She stared at the ground for a good minute, gathering her thoughts.

"I had a dream, an ill omen," she said and looked up at the king. "There was a dark shadow looming over you. Death is near. I feared the worst."

"I'm still quite alive," Dolnar said.

"Yes," Ariastheni nodded slowly, "and so is the dragon you told me was dead."

Sir Bendell jumped from his seat.

"You'll not call the king a liar, regardless of whose kingdom you set forth from!" Sir Bendell shouted. "You'll be put in chains and tortured for such insults!"

"Ben, sit," Dolnar said calmly, setting a hand on his friend's shoulder.

"But sire!" Sir Bendell said and turned to his king. "This witch has insulted you!"

"Have we not been able to pierce the dragon's hide, even though it has fallen?" Dolnar said. "Has its flesh not rotted as a dead beast should? We may profess to know the ways of the normal world, but a dragon has special properties you and I may not understand. A few wise men have proffered the same advice."

Sir Bendell grimaced, recalling his words just moments ago in the broken throne room. He turned and gave Ariastheni a menacing glare.

"You'll keep a civil tongue around his majesty," Sir Bendell growled and sat with a huff.

"I meant no disrespect, your majesty," Ariastheni said and bowed her head in apology. "But..." She raised her head. "Though it appears to have been dealt a mortal blow, it simply hibernates and heals as would a bear through the winter. I know not why, nor why it hasn't moved, but it is still alive."

The royal scribe arrived, sporting a long flowing white beard and wearing a dark red robe.

"You called, your majesty?" he said in a cranky old voice.

"Tellosh, tell me what we know of the trial and execution of the sorcerer Zettelek?" Dolnar asked. "I recall there being something we worried over after his death, but I can't recall the details."

"Oh, the curse?" Tellosh asked.

"That would fit the details we're after, yes," Dolnar said.

"Let me retrieve the records," Tellosh said. "Even though I think I recall it, my memory is a bit fuzzy and it seems the details would be important, yes?"

"Indeed," Dolnar said waving him away. "Best speed, scribe."

Tellosh bowed and turned, running away as fast as his old legs and sandaled feet could carry him.

"Humph," Sir Bendell said. "I'd forgotten about the curse. I was so filled with hatred at Zettelek's actions that I felt contempt at his final words, not believing them at all. I don't remember the details, but when his curse didn't come true... we all forgot about it."

"Seems that he'd send a dragon immediately if that was the curse, possibly to free him before he was executed," Dolnar mused. He turned back to Ariastheni.

"Tell me, why did you never entertain the idea of being my queen?" Dolnar sat back and enjoyed the blush that came to Ariastheni's cheeks as she quickly averted her eyes and looked at the floor.

"Your majesty is too kind," Ariastheni said. "I'm but a simple druid. I could never hold court with you. This is not my world."

"Tell me about your world," Dolnar said.

Ariastheni looked up at Dolnar. She glanced at Sir Bendell who just shrugged his shoulders.

"Well, we commune with nature," Ariastheni began. As she continued to describe her world of trees, healing, praying and caring for animals and the common people who sought her out, her voice lilted back to the sing song voice Dolnar so admired and fell in love with nearly twenty years ago.

"Sounds wonderful," Dolnar said.

"It is, your majesty," Ariastheni blushed again and bowed her head. "But it's not the life for a king, forgive me for saying so."

"I agree," Dolnar said. "Your reasoning is sound."

"Thank you," she replied.

"Sounds dreadfully boring," Sir Bendell murmured.

"Ben," Dolnar said disapprovingly.

The scribe reappeared at the doorway, out of breath, holding a bundle of manuscripts in his grasp.

"Your majesty," Tellosh gasped, out of breath. "With your permission?" He held up the bundle.

"Of course, Tellosh," Dolnar said, waving his hand at the table.

Tellosh stepped forward and dumped the manuscripts on the table. He spread the five sets of papers out and began leafing through them, every once in a while muttering something and then moving on to the next pile. In the middle of the third pile, he slapped his hand down on the page and turned to the king, beaming.

"I've got it!"

King Dolnar smiled and inclined his head forward.

"Oh, of course, your majesty!" Tellosh said and turned back to the page. "It says Zettelek said 'With my death, you will seal the curse and the beast shall hunt and destroy everything you care for until the end of your kingdom.' And then you nodded and Marvin cut off his head."

"Marvin?" Sir Bendell asked.

"Ah, yes, my brother Marvin was the executioner. Unfortunately, he's since passed. Died of consumption while I was away at the monastery studying several years ago."

"The end of my kingdom not my death?" Dolnar asked and stroked his chin.

Tellosh looked back at the manuscript. He traced the words carefully with his fingers. He turned back to Dolnar.

"That's what was recorded and it's accurate if my memory serves," Tellosh said. "All kings reign until their death or so it's been recorded."

"Thank you, Tellosh," Dolnar said. "You may return to your studies."

Tellosh bowed his head, gathered his manuscripts and hobbled out of the room. Ariastheni looked at Dolnar with a sadness that shook the monarch to his core. He chuckled nervously.

"Not to worry, my dear, I'll be abdicating the throne in a fortnight and then we can permanently dispatch the beast where it lay."

The look of sadness did not dissipate, but was accompanied by a shaking of the head. Again, Ariastheni looked at the floor.

"I can only advise, milord, but the beast will be up within a few days' time if not sooner. That wound is nearly fully healed. Even now, I can barely sense the damage and the injury is no longer visible on the dragon's hide."

"We noticed the wound healing," Dolnar sighed. "I remember the day the shaft from the ballista bolt slid from the wound nearly three months ago. The wound has been closing ever since, but we thought it some minor magical trickery. Turns out it wasn't minor at all."

Dolnar looked at Sir Bendell, who had been strangely silent the last few minutes.

"What say you, Ben?"

Sir Bendell looked up with sadness in his eyes as well.

"I can find no fault in your logic, sire, nor that of the maiden druid." Sir Bendell stood up. "I would be the first to advise you to never give up your throne, but under the circumstances, I..." His voice faltered and he found he couldn't finish his sentence.

"It is well, Ben," Dolnar said softly. "Tommy!"

The young runner appeared almost immediately.

"Yes, sire?"

"Tell Sir Frederick, Prince Evan and Lady Drea to attend me at once."

"As you wish, sire!" Tommy bowed and turned on his heels faster than anyone Dolnar had ever seen. He turned to Sir Bendell. "Ben, make the arrangements. The coronation will take place in an hour's time. Have all the people we need, but forgo the decorations. Speed is of the essence."

"Of course, sire." Sir Bendell bowed and headed out immediately.

"You see, Ariastheni, nothing to worry about. In an hour's time, the beast will no longer be protected by this curse and we can dispatch it safely," Dolnar said smiling.

"But, what will you do then?" Ariastheni asked, a look of shock on her face.

"I thought perhaps I might visit the wilds of Oakendell to see what might interest me there," Dolnar said. His low rumble caused Ariastheni to lower her eyes to the ground once more. However, he heard her breath catch at his comment and he smiled.

Sir Frederick was the first to arrive, half in his armor and half out.

"Sire, my apologies, I was just readying myself for some exercises with the men," Sir Frederick said. His woolen trousers hung loose beneath his breastplate of iron.

"I'm abdicating the throne in an hour's time, Frederick," Dolnar said. He held his hand up at the anticipated objection from Sir Frederick which immediately quelled his protest. "The reason the dragon still lies in wait upon our grounds is a curse that can only be broken by me giving up the throne. It's time, Frederick. The ghosts of the past must be laid to rest. As God is my witness, my reign is one of those ghosts."

Sir Frederick nodded. "Your grace, shall I assemble the men for an honor guard for Prince Evan then?"

"Prince Evan shall be attended by no more than ten men. The rest will ready themselves to slay the beast. There's a chance even now that it will awaken before we've completed the coronation. Ready the ballistae. We may have a bit of fighting before the day is done. My last command as king will be to slay that foul serpent with all your might and prowess."

"So it shall be, my liege," Sir Frederick replied and exited hastily.

Prince Evan arrived with Lady Drea in tow. Behind them, Sir Bendell escorted Cardinal Archibald into the room, followed closely behind by Tellosh, carrying another manuscript as well as a pen and quill. All was ready for the signing and ceremony.

Cardinal Archibald approached King Dolnar immediately.

"This is most unusual, your highness. Never before has a king of the realm abdicated," Cardinal Archibald protested.

"Abdicated?" Prince Evan cried out. He immediately strode forth, running his hand through his blonde locks. "Father, this can't be true! I'm not ready!"

"Can either of you fine, upstanding members of society give me a way to end the life of Charos who still haunts our grounds?" King Dolnar said, standing up and thundering in a commanding voice.

A cry rang out down the hall. "The beast moves!"

Ten of Sir Frederick's men arrived to surround and protect Prince Evan.

"Quickly now, while we still have the upper hand!" King Dolnar shouted. "Lady Drea, my apologies. It appears we won't have time for a celebration feast until the beast is slain."

Lady Drea bowed her head and the Cardinal stood before King Dolnar and Prince Evan and repeated the words Tellosh read from a manuscript. Within moments, Dolnar signed the decree, the task had been completed and the former Prince now wore a crown signifying his coronation.

"Be strong, noble and wise, my son. Lead from the heart as well as the head," Dolnar said as he grabbed his son's shoulders and pulled him in for a hug. "Now use that wisdom and get to the safety of the dungeons, my king. Lord knows what this beast has in store for us in its final moments."

The men and the new king rushed away and Dolnar picked up his scabbard from next to the chair. He looked at Sir Bendell and smiled.

"You ready for one last fight at my side, Ben?"

"Always, sir!" Sir Bendell shouted and rushed out after his lord into the night.

THE YEAR THAT WAS

Captain Damien Strontum absently flipped his long pony tail back over his shoulder. His dirty blonde hair was tied up with a piece of fabric similar to the reflective blue tunic he wore. He reached forward and pressed the record button.

"Captain's log January fifteenth, I think. For purposes of keeping track here on Unity, it's the Terran year 2055. I confess I haven't been following the Terran Space Authority guidelines with keeping a log every week, but considering TSA ceased to exist a year ago, I didn't figure I would be in much trouble for it."

Damien paused and took a sip of the hot liquid in his coffee mug. The tea composed of varying spices they could grow in the hydroponics bay tickled his nose. He looked down at the tea and swirled the cup around, causing the tiny leaves floating in it to create a small liquefied tornado. He smiled for a moment and then set the cup down. He looked up at the recording camera.

"Unless something extraordinary happens on our journey, this will likely be my last entry. Beyond leaving a record for whatever intelligent race finds our ship, I don't see the value in making these entries." He cleared his throat as he rubbed his beard thoughtfully. "I know the children aren't going to listen to them."

He leaned back in his chair and looked around the room. "A year ago, something happened on Terra. I thought we'd gotten past war especially after the Mycean outbreak of 2026 that wiped out nearly half the world's population. That event brought a long lasting peace as well as a temporary break to the stress on the planet's resources. Twelve billion people dropped to just under six billion in the space of a few months, but those left behind continued to prosper and breed, so within twenty years, we were again reaching population levels that stretched the resource capabilities on the planet. That's why ships like the Grayson were built. Long range harvesting ships capable of mining and extracting other resources from the asteroid belt and beyond."

Damien looked down again and shook his head. "We had such a bright future ahead of us." He seemed to zone out for a few moments and then blinked rapidly and returned his attention to the camera. "Something happened. Doctor Sheppard—"

A knock on the door interrupted his train of thought.

"Son of a—" he muttered and reached forward to turn off the recording.

He set the drink down on the desk and took the five steps to the door. He opened it and frowned at his second in command, Lieutenant Victoria Driesen. She stood at attention and held up her chin. Her blonde hair was tied up tight in a bun, not a strand out of place. Damien stroked his unruly beard absently, but didn't say anything.

"Sorry, Damien. It all came at once and I felt a little overwhelmed," she said and winced a little.

Damien sighed. It had been a trying voyage to say the least. "What's going on?"

"Emergency beacon has come up for the Tennyson," Victoria replied. "It appears to be drifting and hasn't responded to any hails. There's an atmospheric leak in a rear storage module on the Orion where we were joined. It's already sealed off – nothing perishable in that section. And, Doctor Tanjea has called three times for you in the last hour."

Damien rubbed his eyes and took a deep breath.

"She said she'd just find you on her own, so…"

"So, if you didn't interrupt me, she would've anyway," Damien finished. He stepped out of his room and shut the door. "Let's walk."

Victoria fell into step next to him as they headed to the front of the ship.

"Get Bowers and Simpson on the repairs since they're the ones who connected the ships in the first place. They should be intimately familiar with their own work."

"I've already notified Bowers," she nodded. "Simpson is still, um…"

Damien stopped and Victoria took two more steps before stopping as well. "Okay, it comes into focus a bit better why you came to get me. What's the status of the Tennyson?"

"Just the signal. Weak at first, but stronger as we've locked in on it and maneuvered in that direction. No response to our hails. But we do have a location now. Better than we've had for weeks."

"Set a course to intercept. If she's disabled, we may have to match her trajectory so we can dock. If you can handle that, I can handle Simpson. Get Bowers and his team on that leak. We'll see how the engineering team he's built can handle this. Probably more revealing than test welds in the shop."

"He's been a little gruff with them," Victoria said.

"Our options are cantankerous or drunk. I'll go with

cantankerous for the moment," Damien said. He turned around and headed aft.

"What about Doctor Tanjea?" Victoria shouted.

"I'm certain she'll find me," Damien replied and waved. Victoria turned away and headed back to the bridge.

Damien walked on for maybe two more minutes before he observed a certain brown eyed beauty heading his way. Doctor Illyana Tanjea was on the warpath and he knew why. He slowed his walk as she barreled toward him.

"Damien, why haven't you come in?" she hollered at him before she'd reached him.

"Illyana, so nice to see you," Damien replied.

She came to a stop in front of him and looked up at him. She was six inches shorter than him, but he suspected she could take him in a fight. She wasn't just a brilliant doctor; she was also tough as nails. He looked into her eyes and regretted it almost immediately. He could get lost in those brown pools so quickly.

He smiled and pointed in front of him. "I'm just going to see our resident drunk. Maybe having you along would be good for diagnosis and treatment?"

"Fine," she replied and stepped to the side so he could continue walking. She fell into step next to him.

"I've been busy," Damien started.

"We need to start planning the next generation," she replied. "I've made the lists. We need to review them together."

"It just seems so clinical and sterile," Damien replied.

"We can't treat the future of the human race lightly," Illyana replied. "We can't afford randomness. We need to plan this meticulously."

"But there's no romance, no personal connection," Damien said as he walked. They passed by the hydroponics bay and he glanced in to see several crew members tending to the budding plants growing there.

Illyana grabbed his arm and stopped him. She pointed into the hydroponics bay. "The human race faces the same possible extinction as those plants in there. If not cared for meticulously and planned to the last detail, we'll face the end of our species."

"I prefer to think of humans as a little more complex than plants," Damien chuckled.

"Damien, we need to start soon. Several females are entering their cycle and the time needs to be soon to get this process going."

Damien sighed and resumed his walk. "See, just that. Entering their cycle. You talk like that and it seems so…"

"Scientific?" Illyana replied.

"Detached," Damien replied.

"Look, I know you're feeling loss for Doctor Shepard's passing," Illyana said.

A cloud passed over his face and for a moment he was back on the moon base, going over technical details and smelling her freshly washed hair tied up in a towel. It had taken the sting out of the loss of his family on Earth. In a moment, he recalled the sidelong glances, the smiles and the inevitable hookup in her quarters on the base. They'd found solace in each other's arms even though they had different reasons for doing so.

"We've all lost family and people we care about," Damien said.

"You need to be with Anna Callen tomorrow," Illyana said.

"Our botanist?"

"She has already begun her cycle. There's a small window of opportunity for a successful pregnancy," Illyana said.

"Look, I know we can't store the sperm, but I've said maybe two words to her since she joined the crew from Delta. Isn't there someone I've at least talked to more that I might be better suited for?"

"This isn't about romance, Damien. We have four hundred fifty-nine humans from which to propagate the rest of the species. We have to differentiate our offspring as much as possible to reduce birth defects and maximize—"

"I know why, Illyana. It's just… we're all still human. We're not lab rats." Damien sighed.

"We're going to have to adjust. Our society will need to be comfortable with this for a few generations. At least until we get somewhere permanent to settle."

"This may be our permanent settlement," Damien said.

Illyana looked down. He glanced over and could see her breathing harder than the walk required. He stopped. She stood up tall and wiped her face. On impulse, he pulled her in for a hug and she didn't object.

"We're all human, Illyana. Even you," Damien whispered.

She relaxed into his embrace and cried into his shoulder for a minute.

"I guess I'm just concerned that because we're human, this will lead to some complications of the emotional variety among the crew," Damien said as Illyana sniffled and stepped back.

"We're not designed for space travel, Damien. There's no telling what will happen to us once we've been in space for several generations. It may change us so much we can never go back to a planet's surface."

"That doesn't encourage you to wait?"

"We can't wait. Every moment there's a possibility someone will die and we'll lose that genetic diversity our future may depend on," Illyana said. "Maybe a ship wide conference to explain we can't tie ourselves to antiquated societal norms anymore. Child birth and child rearing will be different for a while, maybe forever. I don't know. I'm sorry, I can explain the technical details, but the emotional aspects are just a little beyond me."

"Well, we may have more diversity to choose from soon. We've found the Tennyson," Damien said.

"You still need to start the process with Anna. We can manipulate genetic diversity with these choices, but we can't choose the sex of the children. We are looking at an uncertain breeding future. It will take a while to obtain and review the genetic profiles of whoever we get when we connect with the Tennyson. Anna should be pregnant before then."

"OK, matchmaker. I'll plan a rendezvous with Anna. Do you think she'll want flowers?"

"She's a botanist. I'm sure she would if we had the capacity to grow such things." Illyana smirked.

"I was thinking of looking up a picture of one," Damien said.

"She may enjoy the thought even if it wouldn't be much of a surprise to show her some of her life's work," Illyana replied.

Damien came to a stop in front of a nondescript door. The number 179 next to it seemed a little dusty. "Hmm, I think we may need to check the air scrubbers," Damien said as he ran his finger along it and collected a small amount of dust. He shrugged his shoulders and knocked on the door. The door opened and a disheveled redhead stared out at them. The reek of alcohol was immediate and overpowering. Damien and Illyana wrinkled their noses.

"Oh, hi, asshole," Alan Simpson said as he gave a flippant salute to Damien. He nodded to Illyana. "And the good doctor." He burped and turned around, walking back to his bunk.

"What the hell do you want?" Alan said as he sat down.

"Ahem, we're concerned about your state of mind. Clearly,

you've been drinking again," Damien said.

"Fuck if I care, asshole. Anything else? I'm busy," he said as he pulled out a small bottle and took a swig.

"How did you even get alcohol?" Illyana asked.

"It's amazing what you can do with a couple potatoes, a little yeast and some sugar. I brewed it back on Delta. Got a couple years worth stashed around the ship. You can stop by for a little nip any time Doc," Alan said and then looked at Damien. "But not you, asshole."

"Alan, you need to stop drinking," Damien said.

Alan jumped up from his bunk. "Or what, asshole?" Alan shouted as he got in Damien's face. "You gonna throw me off the ship, big guy? You already took everything I loved, why not take my life too?"

"You lost her long before I came into the picture because of your drinking," Damien hissed.

"Big man on campus gotta fuck my wife? We still had a shot until you pushed your big cock in her face," Alan growled.

"Jesus, Alan," Damien said. "You become a real charmer when you're drunk."

"Well, it's all I got left, asshole," Alan said. He turned around and slammed the cabin door.

"That seemed to go well," Illyana said as she turned from the cabin and started walking back in the direction they'd come from.

"We're all human. Alan's perhaps more human that any of us," Damien replied.

"I didn't realize Doctor Shepard and he were—" Illyana began. Damien held up a hand.

"They'd been divorced for two years before everything went to hell on Earth," Damien said. "The only one imagining them getting back together was Alan."

"He lost everything in the accident on Delta, then," Illyana said.

"Well, clearly not his precious alcohol. Now I know why he volunteered to recover all the supplies we could gather from Delta after the accident. He must've smuggled it aboard in the legitimate cargo," Damien scratched his head.

"We've all had to adjust to circumstances beyond our experience, Damien," Illyana said. "Alan was an alcoholic, a welder and now a useless piece of the crew."

"You have him setup with someone on board? Maybe a little time in the sack will chill him out. Give him something else to live for," Damien said. "A little sex might break him out of his funk."

"There are side effects to increased alcohol consumption on the male reproductive anatomy," Illyana said. "Given his history and continued consumption, I didn't put him on the list at all. The likelihood of him producing any viable sperm is incredibly low."

"Damn. He really has lost everything."

They came to a fork in the hallway. Illyana nodded to Damien.

"I expect to hear of a successful coupling within twenty four hours," Illyana said.

"Coupling," Damien chuckled. "So romantic."

"Promise me," Illyana said, looking at him sternly. He looked into her eyes and felt that yearning for real connection again. He smiled.

"I promise," Damien replied holding up his hand. "On my honor."

"Good," Illyana said. She turned and walked away. Damien stood there for a moment watching her go and his imagination took a small flight of fancy for a moment.

"I'd hack that list, if I could," Damien murmured. When Illyana had turned another corner out of sight, Damien returned to his progress toward the bridge.

Minutes later, Damien walked onto the bridge to the chatter of technicians and scientists debating the status of their wayward sister ship. Victoria approached him as soon as she had a moment.

"Still no communication with the Tennyson. We've established an approach vector. Should be around twenty-six hours before we get close enough to attempt a docking," Victoria said as she stood at attention.

"At ease, Victoria. We need discipline on board but not that much. How are the repairs going?"

Victoria brightened up at this.

"Mister Bowers is suiting up now with two other maintenance technicians. He said it shouldn't be a problem. This is exactly what they'd been training for."

"Good. I want them back inside before we start any docking procedures with Tennyson. It's going to be complex enough without worrying about losing someone on a space walk."

"Of course. As for the Tennyson, we'd like to use the same remote drones that found the external leak on our own ship to look for any external damage on her as well," Victoria said as she pointed at a visual schematic for a drone on one of the bridge monitors in the science officer's area.

"That's great initiative, Victoria. You're going to make a fine Captain one day." Damien grinned and his second in command noticeably blushed.

"Not any day soon, I hope, sir," she replied with a grin.

"Maybe sooner than you think," Damien said with a sigh. "I'll be heading up the boarding party on the Tennyson. You'll be in charge back here. Space isn't very forgiving. Something goes wrong over there, you may need to make some hard decisions."

The lieutenant looked down for a moment and then back up

at Damien, a firmness present in her face that he hadn't seen before.

"We don't leave our people behind, sir," she stated.

"You do if they're dead and there's nothing to be done," Damien said. "We don't know what's happened on Tennyson. We're going in literally blind. We'll get some ideas on her status from those drones, but not what's going on inside. That's a big mystery. I don't like mysteries in space, but she is chock full of them."

"No argument there," she replied.

"I'm going to go help Bowers if I can. Just keep track of things here and…" Damien frowned. "You know, if you could go tell Simpson he's been selected to be on the Tennyson boarding party that might get him out of his funk. It would be great to get him engaged in something other than his own misery and stashed vodka. Be complimentary, flattering even. He's a valuable asset if we can get him back on track."

"I'll do what I can, sir."

Damien nodded and exited the bridge.

He made a side trip to the hydroponic facility for a short chat with Anna. On the way, Damien mused that it may be the first time he'd ever been with a woman he didn't have to woo and impress in any way. It was a simple scientific transaction for the survival of mankind. So clinical, so detached. Did that make it worse or better?

He entered the module and looked around at the opaque tubs filled with plants. Several people filled the room with varying levels of activity. He watched a young man simply cocking his head quizzically at a tub of greenery and another woman lifting a tray filled with plants and hanging roots while another technician examined clear tubes going into the tub below.

A blonde walked up to him and smiled nervously.

"Captain," she said with bowed her head slightly. "I'm Anna. You're here about our, uh…"

She frowned.

"We need to set an appointment, I'm told within the next day," Damien replied.

"Yes, it's just that," she looked up at him with tears in her eyes. "John's quite upset."

"John?"

"He heard there would be coupling going on and when he found out I was selected…" Anna wrung her hands.

"Are you dating?" Damien asked.

"We've had a few sit downs. We haven't even kissed yet, but… I'm afraid this will mess everything up with him."

"This is a purely biological connection. There's no romance. Not that you're not lovely, but I can assure him I have no designs on continuing a relationship outside of this encounter."

"Well, I'm not sure he's going to just forgive a one night stand or one week or however long this will take."

Damien noticed the dark circles under her eyes.

"You're not alone. This is a big adjustment for everyone. I'll make an announcement."

"He doesn't know it's you," Anna said as she looked down.

Damien gently raised her chin with his fingers. She looked him in the eyes.

"Honesty and openness is going to be more important than ever now. We've only got each other to rely on in a harsh universe. I'll take the worry out of revealing this for you by making it public for everyone. This isn't something that should be hiding in the shadows."

"Are you sure?"

"It's a new day. We can't just do things the old way. We have to adapt or die. Like the plants you take care of every day. They change to accommodate their environment. Change with the times, if you will," Damien smiled grimly.

"But, some people will hate you."

"Some already do," Damien sighed and winked his eye. "I'll see you in eight hours. It will be respectful and only last as long as it needs to."

Anna nodded.

"If it doesn't work out with John, I apologize for that. I wish there was another way, but our resources are limited as you well know."

"I know," Anna said. "I think he does too."

"I'll see you at the announcement hopefully," Damien said and patted her hand gently. He turned and left.

Halfway to the airlocks, Damien located one of the communication terminals. He pressed a button and got a single line comm-link to the bridge.

"Lieutenant, I need you to make an announcement. We'll have a ship wide all hands in two hours. The meeting will be broadcast across the intercom system to essential personnel who can't leave their duty stations."

"What's the subject of the meeting?" Victoria asked.

"Our upcoming rendezvous with the Tennyson and the future of mankind," Damien said.

"Light subject," she replied.

"Funny," Damien laughed. "If you could make the announcement, I'd appreciate it."

"Right away, Captain."

Damien clicked off the comm-link and sighed. He sniffed and turned back to his brief journey to the airlocks.

The ensuing space walk turned out taking more time getting into space and back from space than the actual work on the exterior of the ship. A few bolts had been missed during the original melding of the ships and a strut had come loose, lifting other components out of place. Replacing the bolts, tightening them down and applying some instaseal before welding took care of the issue. The repair wasn't just good as new, but better than new. On the matter of the instaseal product itself, it was one of a number of resources that was finite and irreplaceable. It was yet another factor pushing them to find somewhere habitable in the universe besides their temporary space ship home.

The morale boost for the maintenance crew at having the Captain take a personal interest in their work was a big bonus. It might have been different if the repair hadn't been successful, but for now, the maintenance crew was in good spirits. Considering the potential work ahead of them when they reached the Tennyson, Damien was happy to get their mood and confidence on the plus side.

Even with a few hours and some contention from Doctor Tanjea on his proposals, Damien felt he was ready with his directives for the crew. Truth be told, he wasn't entirely comfortable with them himself.

When the bulk of the crew had assembled in central mess, Victoria patched him into the ship announcement system for his presentation.

"My fellow Unity crewmates, I want to start by thanking you all for sticking with the rest of us through this adjustment period. We're coming on the last phase of assembling our final crew with the upcoming merger with the Tennyson. It's no secret we have a bit of a mystery on our hands with that ship. We haven't had any communication and she appears adrift. Our hope is the crew is fine and they're just having some problems with their systems. Let's just keep that in our minds as we pull up alongside our sister ship and prepare to board. We anticipate joining her within the next day. My request for you to join the boarding party will be coming to you shortly.

"We are on the precipice of a new chapter in humanity's quest for exploration and survival. Earth as we knew it is uninhabitable for probably thousands of years. As such, we've set our course for other possibilities in the cosmos. You and I will never see that brave new world. It will be the legacy of our grandchildren, great grandchildren or some generation beyond that to visit and colonize new destinations.

"We have only ourselves to start this new generation of explorers. As such, we're going to be doing things a bit differently. Our children will be a mix of everyone on board. It's the best way to provide a solid genetic baseline for future generations. In an effort to maximize potential and reduce birth defects, we have generated a system of matching pairs for a single birth. That system will be iterated for as long as each of us is fertile and can continue to contribute to the gene pool. There are only so many of us, so this is a purely scientific basis upon which we're making these selections. It isn't personal, it isn't salacious and it isn't romantic. As a people, we can't afford to cling to those concepts when it comes to childbirth and childrearing. We're literally a village, the last village of mankind and we'll have to join together even as we make sacrifices.

"This doesn't mean you can't pair up as a couple or whatever bond you feel is appropriate. It does mean that children will be created by selection, not romance. We're all going to raise this next generation together. All the children will be everyone's children. We can't afford to approach this any other way.

"As such, I've instructed all pairing selections to be public. There is no reason to keep it a secret. Get used to it. I'm not comfortable with it either, but I see the need to get over it. Reach outside my comfort zone. I only ask that you be respectful and caring when you're performing this duty. It's not how we'd like it to be. It's how it must be.

"Secrets don't help us as a society. Starting in two weeks, we will also make all medical records publicly available. If anyone has medical issues, it won't be a secret. It will also be accommodated where possible so those people can continue their contribution to our society. Until we receive additional crew from the Tennyson, there are only four hundred fifty-nine of us now. We are all we have. Let's be supportive and respectful and we will survive. We are the future of humanity. Thank you."

The murmurs started before he'd even finished, but he wasn't waiting around for discussion. He'd read every personnel file and he knew who the main objectors would likely be. Most of the personnel had a heavy scientific background. He wasn't expecting much resistance from them. The blue collar types were the ones he expected most of the resistance from. Anyone who had formed bonds with someone else on board might very easily get protective, defensive and problematic. On the other side, this was very much a burden on the female crew members. Some of them may indeed be very resistant to being directed to get pregnant and give birth especially with someone not of their own choosing. There were a small number of crew who had sexual identity concerns that would have to be navigated with some care, but he hoped there would be some understanding among them as well. Then, of course, there were those who didn't like being told what to do under any circumstances.

He was a few steps down the hall before he had his first surprise. Silvio Donner, his primary materials research scientist, fell into step beside him.

"Damien, I have some concerns," Silvio said.

"Really, Silvio?" Damien replied as he continued walking, his step even and unhurried.

"It's not typically something I advertise, but I am religious," Silvio stated.

"And?" Damien said. "Do you have a religious objection to our course forward?"

"God intended a man and a woman to be married and faithful to one another," Silvio started.

"Abraham, among others, had multiple wives in the Bible, Silvio. It's not like I haven't thought about this. But tell me, what of God wiping out nearly all of humanity? Seems to me there was a promise of some sort made that he wouldn't do that again." Damien continued his normal pace forward. Silvio seemed to stutter step a bit as he thought about his response as well as trying to maintain pace with Damien.

"It's not right," Silvio responded.

"Silvio, we're very much back at ground zero as a race. Be it like Adam and Eve or after the flood, there are only so many people to go around. If we don't do this with an eye to science, we'll suffer birth defects in a generation or two that may be insurmountable. We're already up against the unknown of conceiving and raising children in space. Sure, we have the rotation of the ship providing a semblance of gravity, but it's not exactly equivalent to Earth's and we're facing other unknowns like cosmic rays among other things. As a scientist, you must realize this is the only rational path forward."

They continued on in silence several hundred feet before they came to a fork.

"I'll have to think on this," Silvio said as he stopped. Damien turned to him and grabbed his shoulders gently.

"This is medical science we're talking about. We can't afford to not think two or three generations ahead with every decision we make. There aren't any do overs. This is it. Do the math. In the Bible, there were unconventional solutions to the number of breeding pairs available to humanity. I'd say our solution isn't anywhere near how controversial that would be to modern day society." Damien smiled.

"It seems wrong," Silvio said.

"I won't argue that," Damien replied. "But we'll have to get beyond our own sense of normality for the good of the human race. Look, none of us ever thought we'd be in this situation. We're doing the best we can with what we've been handed, okay?"

Silvio nodded and gave a grim smile. Damien patted him on the shoulder, gave him a wink and left Silvio standing there as he continued on his way.

Hours later, Damien couldn't believe how nervous he was about the appointment with Anna. After some fumbling and apologies, they eventually were able to get the deed done. He never thought it would be so difficult. Anna was attractive, but there was no doubt she wasn't into it and neither was he. The act was purely physical and even barely that. As he left their appointment, it weighed heavily on him that this situation was going to be more difficult on the crew than he'd ever imagined. He was at a loss how to make it easier. It defied societal norms they'd all grown up with. The relationship triggers were hard wired into their brains.

When he got to his quarters, he took a look at the chronometer on the wall and realized he'd been up for over eighteen hours. The rendezvous with the Tennyson was just a few hours away. He needed some rest. Maybe being well rested would benefit his next appointment with Anna.

When his alarm went off four hours later, he felt like his head had only just hit the pillow. He groaned as he sat up and felt the soreness that had overtaken his body.

"I'm not getting any younger," he whispered as he rubbed his eyes. He took a deep breath and got up. As he dressed, a knock on his door made him sigh.

"Enter," he announced. Victoria opened the door.

"Just wanted to make sure you were awake," she said.

Damien chuckled.

"And when did you sleep last?" Damien asked as he pulled on his shoes.

"I slept for a full eight while you were still up for eighteen hours straight," she replied as she leaned against the door jamb. He noticed her blonde hair was down and flowing around her shoulders. It was a good change.

"Well, I'm glad you can sleep so easily," Damien replied as he stood up.

"Whoever said it was easy?" she replied as she stepped out of the way.

"Well, we don't have much in our supplies that help with sleep," he said as he stepped out into the hallway. Victoria fell into step beside him.

"We've recovered a lot of vodka in the last twelve hours hidden all over the ship," she said with a smirk. "Couldn't resist a little nightcap myself to calm the nerves."

"You trust his brew?" Damien raised his eyebrows as he looked her direction.

"Definitely had it tested beforehand. Plus, since he used Delta supplies to make the illicit brew, I figure that makes it everyone's property," Victoria smiled. "Properly rationed, of course."

"Of course," Damien shook his head. "You know, Victoria, I think you'll make a wonderful Captain after all."

"Thank you," she replied. "But don't go off retiring just yet. We have a few things to tackle together first."

"You're very confident today," Damien replied.

"First coupling," she replied. "It wasn't half bad. He has a really cute ass too."

"I'm glad it went well for you."

"Could've been worse, could've been better, but under the

circumstances," she sighed. "It was a welcome change. Wouldn't have been something I'd have done on my own."

"I'm sorry if you felt used," Damien replied.

"It wasn't that," she frowned. "As someone on the command staff, developing a relationship with someone on board can appear as favoritism. Fraternization has always been looked down on. With this development, I can get a release from those concerns and maybe enjoy myself for once. No attachments, but an outlet for some frustration. Oh, and he enjoyed a bit of vodka as well."

Damien smiled. "At least it will go well for some," Damien turned serious again as they stepped onto the bridge. "How is Tennyson looking?"

"Dana," Victoria said to a woman manning a console a few feet away. "Could you bring us up to speed on the latest with the Tennyson?"

"Yes, sir," Dana Stillson replied. She flipped her long braided hair from in front of her onto her back as she turned to face them. "We've matched Tennyson's rotation and speed. The drones found a cracked window in the command module large enough to vent atmosphere from within."

"From a collision?" Damien asked.

Dana shook her head.

"It appears to have come from within, but with rapid decompression, the origin of the damage is hard to pin down."

Damien nodded.

"Further evaluation of the entire vessel noted no exterior damage," Dana said. She punched a few buttons on her console and the main screen on the bridge lit up with a schematic of the Tennyson. "As far as we can tell, all the other systems would remain intact. There are several bulkheads in place that may have closed to seal off the rest of the ship, but with no way to get help from outside, they may have limited capabilities to repair the damage and rescue themselves.”

Damien walked to the schematic and pointed at several points along the side of the Tennyson.

“These are all egress points from which a spacewalk could’ve been initiated,” Damien turned to Dana. “Why wouldn’t they have utilized them and gotten things repaired?”

“Sabotage,” Anna’s voice stated from the bridge entrance. Everyone in the room turned to look at her.

“That’s a great guess, Doctor Callen,” Damien said hesitantly.

“It’s not a guess,” Anna replied. “Sabotage. I felt it an hour ago.”

“Felt it?” Victoria asked.

Anna looked down. She willed her fingers to stop fidgeting.

“I evidently have latent psychic abilities that have only just surfaced,” she looked at Damien. “A result, I suspect, from activities I’d never engaged in before. It’s not just sabotage, I sense. There’s death, fear and anger as well. Primarily fear.”

“Are the people aboard the ones who committed the sabotage?” Damien asked.

“Captain,” Victoria began to object but Damien just held a hand up.

“We’re in completely new territory in more ways than one, Lieutenant. Any information we can get will be helpful.”

“I don’t think so,” Anna said. “But, I’ve only just begun to handle what’s going on. I can’t be certain.”

“Thank you, Doctor Callen. We’ll take every precaution. You might want to check in with Doctor Tanjea just to be sure everything is okay with you,” Damien nodded his head respectfully toward Anna. She smiled grimly and left.

“Captain,” Victoria said quietly. “It’s not scientific.”

"Not everything is understood as well as we'd like to think, Lieutenant. The universe has many surprises in store for us, I'm sure. We need to prepare for all contingencies we might face on boarding the Tennyson including a hostile reception."

"Well, I can't argue with that under any circumstances." Victoria nodded and turned to Dana. "Let's make sure the entire boarding party has access to this schematic."

"Even Mister Simpson?" Dana asked.

"Especially Mister Simpson. He's going to be in charge of the engineering party," Victoria said.

"Alan Simpson?" Damien asked hesitantly.

"It's amazing what an alcoholic will agree to do if you promise him access to a few bottles of his stash that was confiscated." Victoria smiled.

"I'm going to pin those captain's bars on you myself," Damien murmured so that only Victoria could hear.

Victoria winked at him.

"Boarding party is suiting up. I'll be here waiting for your orders," Victoria nodded, all business once again.

Damien left the bridge.

In the ready room, Damien walked in to find the other ten members of his boarding party suiting up including Alan who looked at him and then shook his head. Damien chalked it up as an improvement that he didn't say anything disparaging. Twenty additional technicians assessed their health, suits and all the interconnecting systems assuring they'd survive their anticipated exposure to the cold vacuum of space.

An hour later, with comms checked and half a dozen members armed with non-lethal weapons as well as tools, the ship extended the connecting tunnel to the Tennyson. Magnetic clamps in place, they disembarked through the large airlock into the tunnel which was void of atmosphere. Alan and two other technicians attached the necessary clamps and pry bars to get the outer doors of the bridge airlock open. Even as they prepared to crack the shell of the other ship, Alan directed the other two technicians back. If there was still pressure inside the ship, it could blow a tool through one of their suits.

Alan ratcheted the mechanical system to open the door just a crack and was relieved there was no burst of atmosphere forcing its way through. The airlock was indeed empty of any air pressure.

The two technicians came back to the door and they pried it the rest of the way open. The process was designed to go slowly to reduce the damage to the internal mechanisms of the airlock door. Once inside the outer airlock, they went through the same process on the inner airlock door to much the same effect. The bridge inside the ship was also empty of atmosphere.

The eleven crew crawled through and the tedious process of sealing the outer door began. While the three engineers worked on the airlock doors, Damien and the rest of the crew ventured throughout the bridge that was a mirror of Grayson and Orion's bridges. With the proper repairs, they'd have three redundant systems to get them through their long journey to an unknown destination.

"Captain," one of the other crew said over the comms. It was Eric Rodriguez, the operations manager from Delta. He'd been a fantastic addition to the crew, helping coordinate the increased resources and personnel. "We've got human corpses here."

Damien looked over and saw the ruptured remains near a science console. They'd been flash frozen in the vacuum of space. It was hard to tell if they'd been dead before the bridge had been compromised.

"Another over here by the breach," Suzanna Breyer said over

the comms. Damien made his way over and noted the scorch marks on the inside of the ship around the breach in the thick window.

"Fire and maybe an explosion," Damien said.

"There's nothing in this console that would have caused this much damage," Suzanna said. She would know. She was one of the original computer scientists on the design team for the bridge systems of these ships.

"Can this be repaired to where it's functional again or are we looking at a bridge full of spare parts?" Damien asked.

"This section is redundant even on board the Tennyson. You can safely seal up this breach, not access any of this equipment and the Tennyson would be fully operational. Assuming..." Suzanna trailed off as she disconnected the diagnostic equipment. She turned away from the console and walked the length of the bridge. She stopped at an unassuming pipe on the wall. Using a screwdriver, she removed a panel from the pipe and attached the diagnostic equipment to it. After a few seconds, she turned to Damien.

"There are no signals between here and the rest of the ship. This bridge is entirely cut off. It's still repairable, but curious. This is why we couldn't talk to the ship. There's no way for the communication array to reach the redundant systems behind the bulkheads."

"Couldn't they use the rear array?"

"Not if they couldn't get out to do a spacewalk," Suzanna said. "It's intentionally disconnected from interior systems to protect it in case of an overload. But it's not designed for a full system disconnect. There are redundant lines running along both sides of the bridge and they've been severed. The rear array has a line on the outside of the ship, but by design it wouldn't be damaged by the kind of systems failure we're seeing here."

"Doesn't seem like a very good backup," Damien said.

"It's not a backup, per se. The system is already designed with a backup which has been disabled. That damage combined with the disconnection of the redundant lines points to intentional sabotage by someone. Possibly that someone who is wedged beneath the command console," Suzanna pointed back toward the front of the bridge.

Damien walked forward and saw a body wedged under the front of the command console directly across from the damaged window. Char marks on the front of their suit suggested they'd been at the window and console when it exploded.

"Suzanna, if you were a saboteur, where would you pick on this bridge to breach the hull?" Damien asked.

"Probably a window at the front of the bridge where there was an unused redundant console I could hide an explosive charge in. But captain, that charge wasn't inside the console. It was detonated on the surface. Someone had to make that happen manually. It would've been noticed otherwise."

Damien looked at the console and again at the figure wedged under the console. He couldn't argue with the assessment. He walked back over to the other two bodies on the bridge. He examined the front of the bodies and then turned them over. One of them had a clear puncture wound in the fabric of their shirt. They'd been stabbed in the back. He was no expert on anatomy, but he figured the injury could've punctured the heart. Death or incapacitation would've been nearly instantaneous.

"Alan, the bridge is a relatively small area. What effect would it have on the rest of the atmosphere in the ship if we sealed the bridge and opened it to the rest of the pressurized ship, assuming the rest of the ship is pressurized?"

Alan stepped forward from inside the airlock.

"We've got the outer airlock door resealed. If the other

bulkheads aren't in place and it's just the one, that's a lot of pressure if it isn't slowly introduced. You could blow out the seal on the window and expose the entire ship to a leak."

Damien nodded. "Well, we better make extra sure our leaks are well sealed. I want to get through that bulkhead and see if there's any crew on here to save." Damien changed frequencies. "Lieutenant, get Doctor Tanjea on the line. I need to assess the danger of slight decompression on the other crew members."

"Of course. Just a moment, she's right here."

There was an audible click and then Doctor Tanjea got on the line. "Captain?"

"Doc, here's the situation. If everything goes according to plan, our sister ship's remaining crewmembers will experience a slight change in atmosphere. The bridge appears to be void of air pressure, but our plan is to seal it. I'm assuming the rest of the ship still has pressure. Will they be able to handle the slight change in pressure or do we need to take additional precautions?"

"There might be some discomfort in their aural canals similar to a drop in pressure from descending a couple hundred feet in altitude. But, it should be temporary and confined to their ears. There should be no other dangers as long as the pressure change is slight. Too much of a change could cause serious rupture of membranes like eyes, but they're generally well suited to slight changes. Just be careful and everything should be fine," Illyana's voice was calm and professional. "Have you contacted the survivors to prepare them?"

"We don't have communication as such," Damien replied. "They may not even realize we're here."

"If they're alive, they know something has changed," Doctor Tanjea replied. "When we connected our ships together, we increased the mass and slightly changed the gravitational properties of our combined ships. There was a little bit of shaking as well. You may not be able to hear anything in space, but inside a ship you can feel these changes and hear the grappling system connecting the ships when they contact the hull. If they're alive, they know someone has at least connected to the ship. Given the timeline of the communication loss… they may not know what happened to Earth. That's more of a concern than their physical well being."

"Yeah, if they've been able to maintain everything else, they have enough food and supplies to survive. If nothing else, they'll assume we're a rescue ship which, in a sense, we are."

Alan stepped up to him and tapped his helmet. "Sorry, Doc. Gotta go. We'll be in touch with our results. We have three dead, so prepare for up to the complement of the ship minus three for medical triage."

"Understood." Damien clicked over his comms. "What is it, Alan?"

"Well, if you're done flirting with the other ship, you'll be happy to know we've got the inner airlock secured and the instaseal is curing. I'm prepping the bulkhead for opening. Same as the outer airlock but with a greater likelihood of an atmospheric burst."

Damien nodded and yawned. "All right. Let's get this show on the road. Thank you." Damien smiled at Alan who just rolled his eyes and turned to walk toward the bulkhead. Damien shrugged. At least they weren't at fisticuffs.

The bulkhead procedure turned out to be less dramatic than anticipated because it was one of several they needed to open. The air inside each sealed section lessened the change experienced by the whole.

After the first bulkhead, the telecommunications and engineering sections there were searched, but found to be empty except for four decomposing bodies. They'd been stabbed as well. They hadn't been exposed to the vacuum of space, but the temperature had been reduced in the section. While the reduced temperatures had slowed the decomposition, it was still clear they'd been dead for a long time.

The next bulkhead opened and the air pressure seemed to even out so there was barely a perception of a change.

"Readings?" Damien said over the comms as he glanced briefly at Maria Chang, the nurse they'd brought to handle casualties and immediate triage if necessary.

"Normal readings for a moderately maintained recirculation system. Breathable, but a bit stagnant," Maria replied glancing at the air sampler in her hand. "Slightly elevated CO_2, but it's breathable and no significant contaminants."

"Let's open up our suits, but keep the weapons handy. We don't know what to expect," Damien said.

It didn't take but a few steps for them to find the unexpected. As they rounded the corner and entered the mess area, a man with months long hair and beard growth dressed in shiny clothing stood up on a makeshift throne at the other side of the room. To either side of him, chained to the sides of the throne, two undernourished women groveled at the base of the throne. Their hair was a tangled mess and they were dirty as well. The chains connected to metal collars around their necks and bands around their wrists. They were otherwise naked.

The shiny dressed man pointed a shaft of wood topped with a long blade.

"You have entered the realm of Jebediah! You are not welcome! Leave at once!" He took two steps down and poked his stick at them threateningly.

"Wilbur?" Alan Simon said as he stepped forward. "What the hell are you doing?"

"Wilbur?" Damien asked.

"Wilbur Dribury. He's one of the Tennyson's cooks. We used to, uh, have a drink now and then."

"This is my domain! Leave now or suffer the consequences!" Wilbur took another two steps down the throne.

"Wilbur, knock it off! This is serious!" Alan shouted.

"I don't go by that name anymore! You've been warned!" The man leaped from the throne and charged them.

"Light him up," Damien said.

Alan shook his head, raised the stun gun and fired. It struck Wilbur and he staggered a bit but kept coming.

"Again," Damien said.

One of the other technicians raised another stun gun and fired. This brought Wilbur to his knees and he dropped the staff.

"Avenge me!" Wilbur shouted before he fell to the ground and shook with the voltage running through him.

The two women at either side of the throne raised their heads and looked up at the ceiling. The tiles that had been a solid mass had been broken up and Damien got a sinking feeling.

"We might have attackers overhead," he advised the crew before the technician who shot Wilbur last suddenly grabbed his neck and fell to the ground with a scream.

Damien caught a hint of movement near one of the tiles and fired his own stun gun. He missed the target, but the leads got tangled with the metal rafters and after a moment there was a scream and a single figure fell from the ceiling to the ground, dropping a small cylindrical weapon. The wiry assailant shakily got up to their feet and stumbled awkwardly trying to escape, but they were disoriented and slammed head first into one of the support poles. They went limp and fell to the floor.

"Sparrow!" Wilbur cried out. He tried to get up, but he was still disoriented by the stun charges.

"How about we restrain Wilbur and see if we can find out what's going on," Damien said.

Maria tended to the fallen technician. She turned to look at Damien and held out a small sliver of wood.

"Careful, this is what hit Jamal in the neck. Probably some kind of tranquilizer. His breathing and stats are stable, but I don't know what kind of long term effect this might have."

Damien carefully took the sliver and held it up.

"Better restrain that other assailant too," Damien said.

"We didn't exactly bring handcuffs," Alan grumbled.

"This isn't exactly the battle mission I signed up for either, Alan," Damien replied. He initiated comms with Unity.

"Unity, we have apprehended two individuals and are evaluating two more for injuries. Jamal has been injured by an apparent tranquilizer dart. We're looking for other survivors," Damien said. He walked over to the two naked women with Suzanna and Maria at his side.

As he approached, the two women shrank back in fear. He stopped. Maria put a hand on his arm.

"Maybe Suzanna and I should talk to them. They have likely been..." Maria trailed off and frowned.

"I understand," Damien said as he looked over at Wilbur lying on the ground. "See if they can tell us where the others are, what happened, anything that can get us answers and find the rest of the crew."

Maria nodded and went with Suzanna to the women.

Damien walked over to Wilbur lying on the ground.

"They're my property! You can't have them!" Wilbur shouted. The battered women cried out, fear still ruling their minds.

"Gag him," Damien grumbled to Alan who was helping the other technician hold Wilbur down.

"I'm the king!" Wilbur shouted before Alan shoved an oily rag in his mouth and tied it off around his unruly head of hair.

"You just lost your crown," Damien replied. He stood up and started to walk toward the other prisoner.

"Guess you've still got yours," Alan grumbled.

"What?" Damien said and turned around.

"You're telling the women what they should do, who they should be with. You're no better than Wilbur here."

Damien paused for a moment and frowned. "It's not the same thing," he said.

"Isn't it?" Alan replied.

"Huh, maybe it is," Damien said. "I think you've earned your drink." Damien turned around and took a deep breath. Was he wrong? He looked over at the women Suzanna and Maria helped as they wrapped shiny emergency blankets around them from the first aid kit.

Was mankind best left to chance and fate? Without free will, what were they trying to preserve?

He looked at the unconscious attacker and then back at Wilbur. "We're the shining future of humanity," he sighed.

An Interview with the Author

When did you start writing and why?

I've been writing stories since before I could even handwrite properly. I remember typing things out on my grandparents IBM Selectric typewriter when I wasn't even in Kindergarten yet. Of course, the stories were likely unintelligible, but that didn't stop me then. Hopefully, it hasn't bled through to my current works.

I always felt I had something to say, stories to tell and bits of my subconscious that were screaming to be shared. I've answered the inexorable call of my psyche to share what is in my head.

Which authors or books influenced you the most as a writer?

Ray Bradbury, J.R.R Tolkien and Robert Heinlein were probably my earliest influences. Bradbury's ability to essentially flow between the genres with his tales has probably influenced me the most in my own storytelling goals. I don't like being pigeonholed into a single genre. It makes marketing a challenge, but it keeps my storytelling consistent with my heart and soul.

Which authors or books had the biggest impact on you as a person?

It's really hard to narrow that down. There are so many different facets of stories and storytellers out there. The breadth of talent and perspectives keeps life interesting and that's reflected in the variety of tales and tellers out there. Honestly, the variety of people who've told their stories and the stories they've told has a bigger impact on me as a person than any single tale or teller. It's shown me that there are possibilities for all writers to share the tales burning within them and that someone out there will likely read and enjoy it. I think that really drives me more as a person and writer than anything else.

Which of your original twelve Prompt stories are you most pleased with?

The Most Dangerous Thing is probably one of my all time favorites. The fall of society with the unexpected twist at the end so nearly mirrors humanity's very real history. I feel it speaks more truth than any other story I've written even as it highlights so many lies.

Which of your original twelve Prompt stories did you find the most difficult to write?

Progression is without a doubt the toughest story. It's more emotional than anything else I've written. While it's not a territory I normally explore, I found it rewarding. It's hard to edit your own story when it brings tears to your eyes.

What book on writing do you recommend?

On Writing: A Memoir of the Craft by Stephen King is one of my favorites. It really gets to the heart of why you write as much as actually crafting the tale.

What advice would you give an unpublished writer?

I didn't truly start to grow as a writer until I joined a writing group and experienced critiques of my writing from other writers. I was a member of one for several years until I eventually reached the point where the critiquers were not giving me worthwhile advice any longer. I had, in a sense, outgrown that stage. It's an important one, though.

When you create that first draft, it's important to do it without a lot of editing. Get the story down, get those elements on the page and empty that story from your mind so it isn't jumping ahead to other parts while you go into your editing. The importance of editing cannot be emphasized more and if you've never experienced critique of your work, can you truly approach it with the idea it can be improved? A writing group let's you know everything can be improved and that first draft is almost never in good enough shape to deliver as is. As your writing experience grows, perhaps the editing becomes less extensive and more of a nuts and bolts spelling and misplaced phrases or words kind of endeavor, but if you've never been critiqued (and never critiqued others), you hardly naturally have the skills for editing.

My first novel, while it went through several self-editing passes, suffered by not having a professional editor go through it. When you've reached the point of novelization, you need another set of eyes to look at what you've put down and honestly help you correct errors you simply can't see because you're too close to it. My first novels had editors that worked with me to correct my own faults. I learned so much from them, as much as I did my first writing group. My current editors are a bit more hands-off, expecting a fully editing final draft product, but I couldn't have gotten to the point of producing that without the layers of editing and critique I'd gotten over the last decade.

Do you have a "dream project" as a writer? What would it be?

I'd probably go with mysteries. I've always been fascinated by the works of Arthur Conan Doyle and Agatha Christie. I'd love to be able to craft a story that gets mystery readers snuggled up on a couch with a cup of hot tea or cocoa reading late into the night wanting to know who the killer is.

The original twelve Prompt stories were written in 2019. In 2020 we all experienced a global pandemic. Did the pandemic impact your writing? How?

I think it has impacted my writing negatively. I get inspiration and energy from others. If I'm not able to be out, socially interacting with others, I feel as if my creativity suffers somewhat. I've found myself watching more television than ever and it is simply because I'm not compelled or inspired to write as much. Some of that may be environmental—my writing computer is in the same room as the television for the family. I can't escape the electronic distraction often. I can't head to the library anymore or the local coffee shop, so getting away from family activities to do serious writing has suffered.